THERE ONCE WAS
A CHILD

THERE ONCE WAS
A CHILD

A Novel

DEBRA WEBB

Edited by Marijane Diodati

Cover Design by Vicki Hinze

PINK HOUSE PRESS
WebbWorks, Madison, Alabama

First Edition April 2018

ISBN-10: 0989904466
ISBN-13: 9780989904469

There once was a child, frightened and alone.

No matter how good the child was, the child was battered and abused.

In time the child grew bigger, stronger and no longer confused.

And then the child was gone, gone...gone.

Until now.

TUESDAY, MAY 1
NASHVILLE

DETECTIVE OLIVIA NEWHOUSE

Positive.

I stare at the pregnancy test stick. My hands shaking, my heart pounding.

Impossible.

Then I look at the other three lined up in a neat row on the marble counter with its double sinks and antique bronze hardware. I *am* pregnant. My eyes close and I move my head from side to side in silent, frantic denial. How could forgetting my pill that one time have culminated in this catastrophic event? In ten years of using birth control products I have been nothing less than diligent. But after my father's unexpected death I was a wreck for a few weeks. Then there was the move…

The excuses tumble through my brain, all of them irrelevant. None of them change the reality. *I'm pregnant.*

Only a little, probably. I had a period last month…it was light, shorter than usual, but I had one. Does that count? So how pregnant can I be? What the hell am I thinking? You can't be just a little pregnant. You're either pregnant or you're not.

I. Am. Pregnant. The words echo through me like shotgun blasts.

A knock on the door jerks my head up.

"Liv, are you going to be awhile in there?"

I suck in a sharp breath, grab up the test sticks and shove them into the back pocket of my navy trousers as I rise from my seat on the side of the tub. I remind myself to stay calm while I shoulder into my favorite khaki jacket—the one I wear basically with everything. I pick up my holstered service weapon and slide it onto my belt, then my cell phone and finally my badge.

I check my reflection. Hair in ponytail, I smooth my hand over a few stray strands. Eyes are clear. No sign of the tears I shed last night. I hate crying. It makes me feel weak. Cheeks are a little pale but that goes with the territory of being a blue-eyed blonde. Good enough, I decide and turn away from the telltale mirror.

Cool, calm and collected. I cannot deal with another fight this morning. Last night's was bad enough. I reach for the door. Except he's being a prick already and I haven't had nearly enough sleep or coffee to function properly.

Even as I remind myself that yelling will not help the situation and most likely won't make me feel any better, I want to do exactly that. There are four other bathrooms in this big ass house for Christ's sake. You would think he could give me five fucking minutes to myself in this one.

Another deep breath. I open the door and brush past him, lips tight in a fake smile. "It's all yours."

I feel his gaze burning a hole in my back as I storm across the bedroom and out the door. It's barely past six. Early for him. The man I'm supposed to marry in November is the president of Brentwood's Neighborhood Bank, one of four local banks his family owns. I don't have to look back to know he's still wearing his Ralph Lauren pajama bottoms, that his dark hair is mussed and his green eyes are bleary with sleep. I also know from experience that he'll wait until I'm halfway down the stairs before he decides on an appropriate display of his irritation. The man takes passive-aggressive to a whole new level.

Annoys the crap out of me. Everything about him used to make me happy. I have no idea when that changed. Or why. But somehow everything feels different, off somehow.

"Good morning to you, too!" he calls loudly. Not quite a shout, mind you. Prestons don't shout. They speak firmly, knowledgeably. They stand their ground.

"Morning," I grumble, uncaring whether or not he hears me.

He doesn't have to hear me to know that I've responded. He has watched my morning rituals

3

daily for nearly a month now and two or three times a week for about six months before that. He understands I'm inevitably behind and that I mutter when I'm annoyed. He recognizes that I am always as tired when I get up as I was when I went to bed because I never, ever manage enough sleep. I'm a cop—a homicide detective. I eat, drink and breathe my work. And sometimes I manage to sleep with the monsters stuck in my head, but not nearly often enough.

And now I'm pregnant.

Charles David Preston, II, fondly called David to prevent any confusion with his father, Charles, was well aware of these facts before he pushed me to move in with him. Before he insisted it was time we progressed to the next level in our relationship and became engaged. I agreed to all his demands, however grudgingly, for no other reason than to make him happy—not because I don't want to be with him or that I don't love him and not even that I'm anything less than as committed as he is. The truth is, I'm not good with change. But I took the plunge into all out rapid-fire commitment...*for him.* Because he wanted to move up the timeline. Because loving him terrifies me on every single level of my being. And because some part of me has suddenly become convinced that I don't deserve him and I despise the idea that he makes me feel so fragile in that regard.

This is why *his* morning ritual bugs the shit out of me.

He dragged me to this new *level* with his eyes wide open. I am not a morning person. I'm an even worse housemate. I might very well be terrible wife material—I'm certain his parents are still in shock over the announcement.

And I am most assuredly not mother material.

Jesus Christ, I'm pregnant.

This is the real problem. I exhale a ragged breath as I shuffle across the kitchen with its gleaming white cabinets and shiny black-and-white diamond patterned floor tiles. From the soaring ceilings to the gleaming wood floors filling most of the luxurious rooms, this classic Belle Meade two-story is every inch the epitome of *his* mother's design style. The furnishings alone likely cost more than I make in three or four years of hard work as a detective. Not to mention his top of the line Mercedes parked in the triple car garage.

This is not my life, it's his and I am not certain I fit into it. How did I not notice this before now?

"What the hell have I done?" I mutter to myself as the panic builds.

My cell shudders against my waist before I can start answering myself. I shove a mug under the coffee dispenser, thrust in the first pod my fingers find and then reach for something else *he* complains about—the amount of attention I give my phone. The truth is, I haven't touched my personal cell phone in ages. It's in a box or a drawer somewhere with zero percent battery life remaining. This is my official work phone issued by the Metropolitan Nashville Police Department.

What am I supposed to do, ignore it?

"Newhouse." I answer without checking the screen so I can push the necessary buttons to prompt the flow of java. I need more caffeine. The two cups I consumed before going on that test-taking spree just didn't get the job done.

Something else to worry about, how much caffeine is safe for a pregnant woman? As it is, my stomach feels queasy already. Can I have morning sickness at this early stage?

I scrub at my forehead and wish away the distant ache. A bad headache is coming. I can feel the storm of it gaining strength. Until a few days ago it had been years since I suffered one of these debilitating migraines, but I recognize the precursors. No one who has ever had that kind of migraine forgets. Even now memories of total darkness, puking my guts out and eviscerating pain flicker in my head like a neon sign with loose mercury. The one that hit me out of the blue the day before yesterday brought me to my knees. I was at the farm, packing a few more things for the big move. When the headache struck I had no choice but to close myself up in my old room and ride it out. Hours passed with me basically unconscious, as if I'd fallen into a deep black hole.

David drove to the farm looking for me in the middle of the night, and found me in the darkness. He stayed with me, uncertain what else to do. As much as I complain, he's a good guy. He loves me.

I know this. He just wants me to be this perfectly organized and perpetually punctual person that I am not. He wants my entire focus when I'm home and that's just not possible. The nature of my work simply won't allow me to separate my personal and professional lives so completely. I am a cop through and through, on and off duty.

Maybe he has suddenly realized this relationship is a mistake and he wants to make me so miserable I'll walk away.

Or maybe it's me subconsciously pushing him away.

Except now it's not just about the two of us.

"Hey, Liv." Walt Duncan, my partner. The gruff sound of his voice drags me back to the here and now, makes me smile. He is the one thing in my life at the moment that feels normal, steady.

"I'm headed your way," he says. "We got a call. Over on Linden Green Drive. Might be just a missing person but there's a lot of blood according to the uniforms on the scene."

I drag my steaming mug from under the dispenser. "I'll be waiting on the porch."

As I head for the front door David pauses at the bottom of the stairs, that *caught you* expression on his face. A sigh drains out of me. This—being here, being *us*—is suddenly, utterly exhausting.

"So you're leaving? Now? No breakfast? Not even a minute or two for quality time with me?"

I am leaving and I cannot eat for fear of vomiting. If I mention the latter, there will only be more questions. "Got a call. I have to go. I don't have a nine-to-five job, David. You know this. I don't understand why my work is suddenly such a sticking point for you, but this is what I do."

His lips compress for a second, then two while he searches for a different strategy. Christ, I know him so well.

I love so many things about him. Why has everything suddenly changed? Why are we both suddenly so determined to torture each other?

"What about all these boxes, Liv?" He gestures to the pile a few feet away. "Are you ever going to unpack and actually start living here or is this nothing more than the new place where you shower and sleep?"

I consider the stack of boxes I reluctantly packed and moved from the farm where I grew up to his stately foyer right here in Belle Meade where so many of Nashville's rich and famous reside. The boxes do sort of block the view into the dining room. The drab brown color certainly clashes with the elegant décor. I'm certain it drives him crazy. Not to mention the unsightly mound of cardboard is the first thing anyone who drops by sees. Appearances are a true sticking point in our relationship. Since moving in I've come to see that everything always, always has to be just so. He thrives on hosting elaborate dinner parties and attending all the right social functions. I don't know why I didn't notice this before I said yes. Maybe because I am rarely more than a drive-by at any of his grand social gatherings. Work always got in the way and he didn't seem to mind. Now he minds. Everything I do is wrong.

This morning, however, the boxes are merely something to use as fuel for a fight. He can't really yell at me for doing my job.

Not fair, Liv. You aren't exactly making any of this easy.

I look into his green eyes—the eyes that charmed the pants right off me the first night we met—and remind myself that I love this man. I plan to spend the rest of my life with this man. Evidently, I will be bearing his child.

Guilt straddles my shoulders so I walk over to him, go up on tiptoe and give him a peck on the cheek. "I'll make it up to you, I promise. And I will unpack the boxes. Soon. See you later. Gotta go."

Then I walk out the door.

He says nothing. He's pissed.

But I'm the one who's pregnant.

A couple minutes later Walt's Tahoe enters the u-shaped drive and stops in front of the house. I hustle down the steps, leaving my mug on the porch. I'll hear about that decision tonight but I have no desire to go back inside and continue the fight that actually started last night—which is exactly what would happen. I want to delay the wedding from the day after Thanksgiving until April of next year. I told him I needed more time. Clearly, we both do.

Of course that was before the pregnancy tests I took this morning, all four of which I tucked inside a trash bag in the bin next to the garage while I waited for Walt. It's not that I don't like kids and don't want any of my own. It's not even that I don't want to get married. I'm just not certain now is the right time. This year has been insane. My father died not even three months ago, the month before that I turned thirty. On top of those life-altering events I agreed to marry the man I love and move into his house—into *his* life. I feel as if *my* life is spinning out of control. All I want is to slow things down a bit.

Except now the timeline is completely out of my control.

The throb in my skull deepens as I climb into the passenger seat and reach for the safety belt. I push away the madness of my personal life and study my partner as he guides his SUV away from the house.

"You look like I feel," I warn.

He glances at me, his eyes bloodshot, his face haggard. "I wouldn't wish that on my worst enemy."

I breathe a laugh. "Me, either."

I continue my scrutiny of him as he drives through the damp streets. Apparently it rained after I went to bed about two this morning. Walt left the office a little while before me. I finalized our reports on the now closed homicide case that kept us beating the bushes for almost two weeks.

Based on those bloodshot eyes of his I think maybe Walt's old buddy JD kept him up a while. That happens a lot lately. I don't ask. If he wanted me to know whatever's going on he would tell me. This is a concept my fiancé doesn't grasp and certainly cannot appreciate. Walt and I—though separated in age by three decades—completely understand each other. We respect each other. There's no "*ball* room" in our relationship. It doesn't matter to Walt that I'm female or that I'm half his age. We're equal. Of course, I'm well aware he's the experienced detective of thirty-odd years and I'm the newbie with only two under my belt, but he never flaunts that detail. He treats me as a peer in every way.

"Jack can be a real ass kicker the morning after." I turn forward and sink into the seat. Walt's a grown man, turned sixty on his last birthday. If he decides to drink more than usual—far more frequently than is normal for him—it's none of my business. I don't doubt his ability to have my back for a second. He's the best. I just worry about him, that's all. Since his wife died, he's had a hard time dealing with life outside of work.

"What's your excuse?" He flashes me a quick grin.

"Trust me." I fold my arms over my middle as if I fear he might be able to see the answer without me saying a word. "You do not want to go there."

"More trouble in paradise?" He chuckles. "I'm not sure your fiancé knows what he's getting himself into marrying a dedicated cop like you."

I grunt. I have no desire to discuss my personal life this morning. Way too complicated. "So what've we got?"

"Uniforms were dispatched for a welfare check. They arrived and found the back door open, nobody home and a considerable amount of blood in the kitchen so here we go." He shrugs. "No big surprise considering the neighborhood. We've worked the area before. Last October, if memory serves."

I remember. Last time it took a week to determine that the wife was the killer. The diminutive woman hadn't looked like a killer. The vic was a big guy—six four, two hundred plus pounds—a drug dealer. The wife had waited until he was passed out on the couch one night, and then put a bullet in the back of his skull with his own backup piece, a .22. Discovering that fact might have been a fairly easy step had she not worn elbow length rubber gloves to prevent any risk of gunpowder residue on her skin. To be completely certain she covered her tracks, she even went so far as to burn the clothes she'd been wearing at the time. Then she claimed she had spent the entire night at her sister's. The whole family backed up her alibi. But by day seven she came forward and confessed. Said it was her Catholic guilt. She ended up getting a plea deal for providing information on her husband's drug connections.

I consider Walt's comments about the scene where we're headed. No body but lots of blood. "Could be the vic is in the ER after cutting him or herself with a knife." Seems a reasonable possibility. "If the blood's in the kitchen, might be nothing but an accident during meal prep."

"I guess we'll see."

"We will indeed." Nothing takes your mind off your personal problems like a potential homicide.

By the time we reach Linden Green Drive the distant ache in my skull has become a throb on the left side of my brain and black spots float in front of my eyes. Not a good sign. The shit storm is coming. My hope is that I can delay the inevitable until we get through this scene.

One side of the yard in front of the gray duplex is cordoned off by yellow crime scene tape that ninety-degrees at the far end and continues on around to the backdoor, I estimate. A police cruiser sits in the driveway behind a rusty white Corolla that presumably belongs to the vic. A white van sporting the blue Metro Crime Scene Unit logo is parked on the grass at the edge of the street. Along both sides of the block, curious neighbors have ventured out into their yards to watch the evolving show. Probably the movie of the week around here—a rerun of last year's classic *Death of a Drug Dealer*.

"Nice place," Walt comments.

I glance around at the trash in the yard, the old, tattered sofa on the porch of the potential vic's place of residence. "Yeah."

A car sits on blocks in a neighboring yard, various parts have been stripped from the metal carcass. Trash is scattered about and banked against the trees on the opposite side of the street. The power lines sag and the pole nearest the crime scene looks ready to fall over. An empty doghouse sits to the right of the driveway, the bald ground around it suggesting an animal was recently chained there.

I hate when people chain up dogs.

We park on the opposite side of the street, next to the tree line. As Walt said, we've been here before. Two houses down is where the drug dealer was murdered the last time we were called to this block. Evidently someone new lives there now. A little girl with curly brown hair hides behind her mother's legs. I wonder if the mother realizes that a man was murdered in the house where she now resides? Definitely not the kind of place where you want to raise a kid, if you have a choice. Not that I know one damned thing about raising kids.

I exile the thought.

Officer Sean Little meets us at the yellow perimeter. The starched creases in his inspection-ready uniform make me feel like a dirt bag. My trousers and shirt are clean but they haven't seen a crease since the last time I bothered with a dry cleaner. Like me, Walt wears his favorite jacket, a navy one that matches his trousers. Unlike me, my partner always wears cowboy boots. Not just any boots either. Lucchese, handmade boots. Over the years he's become known as the "cowboy detective." Nashville loves Detective Walter Duncan. Me, I'll stick with my flat-heeled, rubber-soled ankle boots. You won't catch me in heels like the detectives on TV or in the movies. Being a cop is rarely glamorous work.

Officer Little nods a greeting and says, "Crime scene investigators just got here."

I don't have to ask if Walt called the CSI guys. He prefers to get them rolling rather than waiting until he's on the scene to make the call. Typically we show up about the same time, which works out for everyone. We have a look and they do their thing with no delay in the process.

"Any of the neighbors see anything?" Walt asks.

"If anyone did, they're not talking."

I lag behind as we cross the yard and climb the two steps to the front door. Once inside the small living room we drag on gloves. I force my sluggish brain to inventory the space. Battered sofa is the only seating in the room. An ancient box style television is tuned to some morning show, the poor cable connection making the screen all fuzzy. The television sits on a scarred wooden table. Fake wood floor is dark enough in color to hide how dirty it likely is. Popcorn ceiling is a dingy yellow, an unpleasant match to the discolored blind closed tight on the one window in the room.

The headache is raging now. My vision is starting to blur, damn it. I've never had one of these headaches on duty. Why, after all this time, are they back? After years of no migraines I can't believe another one is happening scarcely forty-eight hours after the last. I close my eyes for a moment and try to slow my plunge toward hell. The dank odor of human filth and the underlying metallic scent of blood have my gut roiling in protest.

"You okay, Liv?"

I snap my eyes open and bring my partner's worried face into focus. "Migraine. I'll muddle through."

"The volume on the TV was turned all the way up when I got here," Little says. "I turned it down. The other side of the duplex is vacant so no one noticed the racket. The guy who lives here didn't show up for an appointment with his attorney."

He flips to a different page in his field notebook. "One Alexander Cagle. So Cagle called in and asked for a welfare check. Back door was ajar when we arrived. There's a bedroom with nothing but a mattress on the floor and a small bathroom down the hall. Kitchen's straight through that doorway." Little gestures to the cased opening beyond the sofa.

Walt and I enter the kitchen where a crime scene investigator is doing his thing. A sizeable pattern of blood has coagulated on the faded blue linoleum. There's a wad of cloth, maybe a washcloth or a hand towel, in the middle of it. No other readily visible signs of a struggle.

"Obvious forced entry at back door," Little says. "The perp appears to have encountered the victim at the sink. Since none of the neighbors heard a gunshot and we haven't found any indication a weapon was discharged in the room, I'm thinking he used a knife."

"Could be the perp had a gun," Walt offers. "If the vic was washing dishes, he may have tried to defend himself with a knife or some other sharp object readily available." He gestures to the dishes soaking in the cloudy water in the sink. "Perp didn't want to fire the weapon and risk disturbing the neighbors so they battled it out. Someone was injured."

As the two discuss the possible scenarios, their words keep time with the throb in my skull and the events play out in my brain like snatches of some low-budget slasher film showing in a dark, sketchy theatre.

Walt asks, "You have an ID on the possible vic?"

"We're assuming it's the guy who lives here. Just moved in about a month ago. Joseph Fanning, that pedophile who was released last month. He was all over the news for a couple of days."

"You should go back to the car," my partner murmurs.

I realize Walt is speaking to me and I force my eyes open. Hadn't noticed they had closed. "I'm okay." Except I'm not, not really.

In fact, I'm a long ass way from okay. I'm pretty sure I'm going to puke any second and the smell of the blood isn't helping. Staying vertical is growing more questionable by the second. I can only see half of my partner's face as he stares at me, worry marring his features. The visual disturbances have begun in earnest. There will be no slowing down the inevitable or the momentum now.

"Officer Little, make sure Detective Newhouse gets back to my vehicle. I'll take care of things in here."

If I weren't afraid the coffee I drank this morning would spew out all over my partner's beloved boots I would open my mouth and argue with him. Instead, I stumble back outside, puke halfway across the driveway for all the nosy neighbors to see, and then climb into the Tahoe.

I close my eyes and slip into the darkness closing in on me.

Sleep is the only way to escape this hellish nightmare.

DETECTIVE WALTER DUNCAN

I hate this place.

It's the same clinic where I brought my wife after she was diagnosed with cancer. The same place I came to and received my own death sentence just two weeks ago.

I hate the medicinal smell. Despise the flowery print of the paper on the accent wall in the lobby. Can't get comfortable in the burgundy upholstered chairs that remind me of the endless vials of blood they suck from my body like vampires. I'll bet they didn't think about blood when they chose the color, they were probably too focused on matching the jewel tones of the accent wall. I wouldn't have known it was called an accent wall if my wife hadn't told me. She always wanted an accent wall in our living room, she'd said. Surprised, I told her I didn't recall her ever mentioning such a thing. I would gladly have papered a single wall for her.

By then there wasn't time for her accent wall.

Maybe that's why I'd rather look at just about anything other than that damn accent wall in this damn lobby. Appointment after appointment you sit in this lobby, watch the same tired, pain-filled faces until one day you come for an appointment and one of those faces is gone. Next time it's another one. Then a new face appears. After a while, you come to realize one thing with complete certainty: soon it will be your face that doesn't show for a scheduled appointment. You'll be the one who died since the last appointment; the one who was planted over at Woodlawn or Spring Hill.

A nurse appears and calls my name. I stand and follow her through the door and then down a long sterile corridor. She weighs me, checks my blood pressure then smiles and leaves me waiting in a plastic chair in this all white room with its cold stainless steel surfaces and wrinkled copies of last year's magazines.

I hate this place.

There are other oncologists in this city. I guess I could have gone somewhere else but what's the point? I'm dying. Might as well take the easy route. This clinic is closer to my house. I know the staff. Know what to expect. I also fully grasp why I've found myself at this place—smoking.

Lung cancer. Terminal. The Pall Malls I smoked for thirty-five years will now claim a second victim.

First it was Stella, my precious wife who never smoked a cigarette even once in her life. My second-hand smoke killed her. She swore it wasn't me. Her father had smoked, too, she reminded me. Died at the ripe old age of eighty-one still puffing on those unfiltered Camels. Stella insisted her lungs were already damaged before she and I ever met. Between the Camels and the coal the family had used to heat their home when she was a kid, she was doomed from birth, she insisted. None of that changes the fact that it is me I blame. I was the one she lived with for thirty-five years of her life. She only lived with her father for twenty-two. I'm the one who killed her. Just like I've killed myself as surely as if I stuck my service weapon to my temple and pulled the trigger.

And all this time I thought I was a pretty smart guy.

When the doc delivered the bad news two weeks ago, he urged me to immediately begin the treatments to try and slow down the progression. That was the route my sweet Stella chose. Fury tightens my lips. And for what? The chemo treatments made her so damn sick. Her beautiful hair turned pure white and then it all fell out. She wasted away to skin and bone. In the end, the treatments didn't slow down the progression one little bit. The only result was the additional misery she suffered the final days of her life. All that extra pain and torment for nothing. She died in three months just as the doc had speculated when he first gave us the bad news.

Why the hell would I repeat the same steps and expect a different outcome? Isn't that the very definition of insanity?

It works differently for different people, the doc assured me when I made that profound statement to him. We can't know if you don't try, he counseled at my initial visit after all the tests. The treatments could add months, perhaps even a year to my life expectancy. The part he didn't mention—even if I did gain some extra time—was the cost. Not the financial cost. My health insurance covers most everything. It's the cost in quality of life that rules out the possibility, in my opinion, and right now that's the only one that counts. I am alone in the world. Stella and I never had children and with her gone, I have no one else to consider.

I think of Liv and feel instantly contrite. But I wouldn't be doing Liv any favors by dragging this out. She would only feel obligated to take care of me. I don't want to put that on her. She has enough on her plate. I remember how she took care of me after Stella died. Liv had just made detective and landed me as a partner around the time Stella was diagnosed. I wasn't fit for duty, I recognize that now, but I couldn't stay at home. Liv held me up, covered for my fumbles and watched my back until I was myself again.

Hell no. I will not shovel more worries onto Liv's back and I will not be a guinea pig for this clinic's research.

I'm dying. Game over.

No retiring in two years and moving down to Florida to go into the PI business with my former partner. I shake my head. Bob Stack and I were partners for nearly as long as Stella and I were married. God, I miss that woman. Miss Bob, too. Liv is a good partner, though. I just hope she makes the right decision where this knuckleheaded fiancé of hers is concerned. I don't like him. He might be rich and from one of Nashville's most prestigious families, but that doesn't make him right for her. The truth is they couldn't be more different. It wouldn't be so bad if he didn't keep trying to change her.

I don't claim to have all the answers, but I do know that when you love someone, you love flaws and all.

While I wait for the doc to go one more round in trying to convince me to give the treatments a shot, I stand, stretch my back, and exhale a blast of impatience. Eventually I take the three steps across the exam room to stare at the vivid illustration of the human lungs mounted on the wall. Too bad mine no longer look anything like that. More in the range of black tar pits.

Finally, I sit back down and mull over the list Liv and I discussed as I drove her home. Poor kid. I've never seen anyone suffer so with a headache. My wife's sister had migraines. I remember she'd have to go into a dark room for the whole day if one started. She had them consistently every month her whole life but she never talked about how awful they were. I see how hard the headaches are for Liv. Crazy part is that until a few days ago she hadn't suffered one in years. I hope they aren't back to stay. No one should have to live with that kind of gorilla in the corner, ready to attack at the worst possible moment.

Personally, I think it's the stress. Hell, her daddy died just a couple of months ago. He was the only family she had left. She's damn young to be in the same boat with me, all alone in the world. Well, she has that fiancé but I'm not so sure about him. I keep that part to myself though. She has to make up her own mind about how she wants to spend the rest of her life.

She's noticed that I'm off my game. I hope I'm not piling more onto her stress level. Even before I got the cancer diagnosis I could be a pain in the ass sometimes. She pretends not to notice. I've been a cop for a long time. I have certain routines and ways of doing things. She appreciates my experience and I appreciate her, period. She's a good girl and deserves better than to be arm candy for some rich boy who thinks he's God's gift to women.

None of my business, I remind myself. I don't even know the guy that well, but I know his type. Full of himself. Wants to rule his little piece of the world. I got news for the guy, Liv won't be ruled by him. Not for long anyway. She'll see the light and then Mr. Fancy Pants will be history.

This case adds another layer of stress to both our lives. Fanning, the probable vic, is a newly released pedophile whose victims were mostly little girls. The bastard is a couple years older than me and the thirteen plus years he spent in prison wasn't nearly enough. God only knows how many children he abused before he got caught. Personally, I hope someone dragged him out into the woods some-where and beat the shit out of him before pouring gasoline over his naked body and setting him on fire. Enough said.

Except, now he's Metro's problem. No matter that he is a monster, not worthy of the air he breathes, the man did his time. He's entitled to the same protection under the law as anyone else. I roll my eyes and heave a weary breath. It's Liv's and my job to make sure the investigation is handled by the book. The chief already called and warned me that the world will be watching to see that the no good SOB—my words, not the chief's—gets the same treatment as any other citizen of our fair city.

Right after lunch I started assessing the list Liv and I had compiled. Pulled up most of the recent addresses and places of employment for each name. Hopefully, Liv will be back tomorrow and we can knock out that list in a couple of days unless we run into trouble locating one or more. The info found in the various databases we can access is sometimes out of date. But we'll find each and every one of them however long it takes. So far, that appears to be the best starting place.

Seventeen. That was the number of families who came forward—the number of kids Fanning was accused of sexually molesting, but it was the last one he lured into his car who nailed his ass to the wall. The other cases were difficult to prosecute since they had no evidence beyond the victim's testimony and a few were beyond the statute of limitations. Ultimately it was that last kid who made the difference. His is the first name on the list and the only male victim.

Mario Sanchez, twenty-five now. He was ten at the time of the abduction. He escaped, nearly killing Fanning in the process.

Too bad he didn't.

I visited Sanchez's mother this afternoon. She showed me his high school and college graduation pictures. He's an engineer now, working toward a second degree in architecture, with a wife and their first child on the way. I called his wife, too. She is visiting her folks in Memphis for a few days. She stated that her husband and a couple of his buddies are on a mountain climbing expedition in Mexico and won't be back until Sunday. She gave me the names of his two friends so I could verify his whereabouts. I didn't get around to doing that part since I had this damn appointment.

I check my Timex. Quarter to five. My appointment was at four-thirty. Another breath of frustration heaves from my chest. Then I cough until I lose my breath. My heart pounds and my face burns with the rush of blood there. When I can breathe again, I wipe my mouth with my shirtsleeve and struggle to slow my frantic heart.

These episodes are coming more often. The pain's a little worse this week but I have to be careful of the medication. I can't be impaired on the job. Liv deserves a partner who won't let her down. If it gets to the point where I feel I can't be a good partner I'll have to go ahead and retire.

Until then, I plan to do my job. I intend to keep this ugly reality to myself. I don't want anyone feeling sorry for me or hovering over me. Work is what I do, it's who I am and I want to keep doing it until I either die or fall down and can't get back up. Then we'll all know I'm done.

Maybe it's selfish but it's how I want to do this.

First thing tomorrow Liv and I will do what we can to confirm Sanchez's whereabouts and then we'll move on to the next name on the list. It's always possible that someone besides one of his victims broke into Fanning's home, fought with him over drugs or some other unsavory business and then carried him off, but it's far more likely that the motive is revenge for the bastard's very public sins. Either a victim or a friend or family member of a victim is the most realistic scenario.

In my experience it's always best to start with the things we know. If none of those things pan out, then we delve into the unknowns. None of his neighbors noticed any visitors at Fanning's duplex. Of course he only moved in one month ago and most of the neighbors prefer not to get involved. No drugs or drug paraphernalia were found on the premises. No alcohol, no firearms. Three pairs of jeans and three shirts in the closet. The same number of t-shirts and boxers as well as socks were tucked into a drawer in a single, shabby dresser. Cheese and deli meats along with a carton of milk were in the fridge. His wallet, cash and ID still inside, was on the bedside table.

I figure if he isn't dead already he will be very soon.

Unless we can find him first.

The door opens and I sit up a little straighter as Dr. Kingsley rushes in, his nurse right on his heels. Kingsley is around fifty, tall, athletic looking. Gray has invaded his hair at the temples. Damn stuff took over mine ages ago.

"Detective Duncan." He glances up from my medical file and smiles. "Have you had time to think about what we discussed?"

He settles onto the wheeled stool and tucks my file under his arm. His hands settle on his thighs and he watches me from behind wire-rimmed glasses as I hesitate before answering his question. He's a doctor, a good one. I'm certain his Hippocratic Oath means as much to him as my vow to serve and protect does to me. But I'm the one who's dying. We'll do this my way.

"I think we'll just let this thing happen naturally," I say. When he continues to stare at me as if waiting for more, I shrug. "I don't want to go through what my Stella went through. I'll just carry on until I can't."

The moment of silence that follows feels like an endless waterfall and I'm already over the edge but the water just keeps crashing down, threatening to drag me into its dark depths.

Finally, Kingsley nods once and passes my file to the nurse standing by. "All right then. Where are we with the pain level?"

We discuss my pain management needs and then he pushes to his feet. I do the same. He extends his hand and I give it an appreciative shake.

"Don't hesitate to call the office if you need anything else," he urges. "You know there will come a time when you'll need help. Start working on that now, while you're still able."

I know what he means. The next unpleasant level to this nightmare: *Hospice.* I nod. "Sure thing, Doc."

I leave with my new prescription. If I'm not dead in three months I have to come back in for a renewal. As I walk through the lobby I wonder which one of those faces won't be here this time next week or the week after that.

In the parking lot my cell vibrates against my hip. I pull it free of my utility belt as I slide behind the wheel of my Tahoe. "Duncan."

"Hey, Walt."

Tim Reynolds from the crime lab. Reynolds is my go to guy. A couple years younger than me, he has more experience and expertise in his little finger than most have in their entire beings. If there's anything in the collected evidence to help our investigation, he will find it. "What've you got for me, Reynolds?"

It's too early to have a DNA match on the blood. We're operating under the assumption that the blood is Fanning's but it's always possible it belongs to someone else. Not the sort of news I want to hear considering what that would likely mean. I want the blood to be his.

"Most of the blood is B Positive, Fanning's type. We should have DNA results in a couple of days. The chief put a rush on it."

"Thanks for the update." The idea that he said *most* nudges me but before I can ask, he says, "Wait, there's more."

I hesitate before backing out of the parking slot. "I'm listening."

"I found a second blood type in the mix, mostly on the hand towel that was in the puddle. This one's O Positive. Maybe that blood was already on the towel before whatever happened in his kitchen. Either way it belongs to someone besides Fanning."

Holy shit.

"Thanks, Reynolds. Let me know the second you find any DNA matches in the database."

Well now. I sag in my seat. If Fanning is a victim, the perp was injured as well during their struggle. The other option is unthinkable. I don't want to go there, but I have no choice.

If the second blood type doesn't belong to the person who injured and abducted Fanning, then what we have is a pedophile on the loose that has injured—possibly murdered—a victim.

Every victim Joseph Fanning ever took was a child.

My gut twists. I need to look at any children who've gone missing in the past few days.

Son of a bitch.

THE CHILD

The bleeding has stopped. I should bandage the wound, but I won't. It's more painful if I leave it gapping open just as it is. Let him suffer.

Most people think I'm a good person but if they knew the real me, they wouldn't like me very much. They see what I want them to see. They know what I want them to know. They have no idea the things I've done. Bad things. But, like everything else in life, my actions are relative. Relative to the pain and the fear. Relative to what *he* did to me for eight long years.

Relative to survival.

I hope they never know how that feels.

The truth is we all have a *then* and a *now*. Sometimes life forces you back to the then. It's never pretty when that happens. No one likes to go back.

So I'm here, in my *then*, and there is no alternative choice. *He* invaded my *now*, dragging me back here. After what he did to me, revenge is the only possible ending. But first, I want *him* to remember every depraved moment of our time together. I want *him* to feel what *I* felt.

And then I want him to die.

There are those who will completely understand how I feel even without knowing the grizzly details. There are others who even if they knew every single horror I suffered would say he is still a human being. All human beings deserve mercy, forgiveness, do they not?

They are wrong. He is not a human being. He is a monster. He is evil. He is going to die soon, but first he is going to suffer.

After all, he started this, *then and now.*

I was seven years old when he took me.

My family wasn't one of those storybook tales that you see on television or in the movies. I don't even know their names. My mother was a junkie. But first and foremost, she was a prostitute. My father was her pimp but when he got too messed up with drugs himself, the two of them threw in together to survive. He used her and she used him.

Neither really noticed me until the day I became the sole remaining viable asset within their pathetic reach.

At the time I didn't realize that my family was different from others. I had never gone to school. I spent most of my days on street corners with my mom begging for whatever pennies passersby would toss us. Sometimes it was enough to feed us—assuming it covered their drug needs and there was money left over. Around holidays was the best time. People felt sorry for me during those periods. They always gave extra. One lady came back with a teddy bear. Soft and wooly. That was the only toy I ever owned.

The year I turned seven, my mother died of an overdose. I felt bad about it. Not in the same way most kids grieve when a parent dies because we never had that sort of bond. But I cried and I missed her for a while. Dad made a new cardboard sign and sat on the street corners with me. He called himself a disabled vet and single parent. I didn't understand what it meant but it worked.

But then something different happened. A man stopped to talk to my father. He didn't want to give us money. He wanted to buy *me*.

At first my dad was like "No way!" But the man just kept coming back and finally my dad said yes. He patted me on the head and walked away, leaving me with this stranger.

The man's name was Joseph Fanning. I didn't comprehend how unfortunate the situation was at the time but I learned very quickly.

Joe, as he liked to be called, was a very bad man. He pretended to be nice at first. He bought me new clothes. He had plenty of food in his dumpy little place—even ice cream. I had only tasted ice cream once.

I had lived in cardboard boxes under overpasses, in alleys next to dumpsters and once in a while in motel rooms or ramshackle apartments for a few days before we were kicked out. In winter, I was always cold. But my new home was warm when the weather was cold. The air conditioning sucked, but it was more important to have heat in the winter anyway.

In that way I guess you could say my life improved. I still didn't go to school and there was no television. Not that I'd ever had a television, but some of the friends my parents would dump me with often had televisions. There were books in my new home. Joe liked reading. I asked him about his books once but he said I didn't need to know how to read. It was best if I stayed exactly as I was…exactly the way he wanted me.

He called me the child, never by my name. He said I didn't have a name anymore and after a while I couldn't remember it anyway. There was a big old trunk in his bedroom and that's where he put me whenever he had to go out alone. It was dark inside and I always worried that the air holes wouldn't let enough air in. At least I had my teddy bear. I gave it a name but I don't remember now what it was. Probably some name I heard on the street or from one of my parents' friends.

Eventually I became too big for the trunk so he built a box for me. It reminded me of the boxes they put dead people in before they put them in the ground. I once saw this on a television in one of the houses where I was abandoned while my parents did some bad thing to get their next hit. I guess, at the time, I had never really thought about what happened to a person once they died.

Soon the possibility of death would become very appealing to me.

In the beginning the things he did to me hurt really badly. I cried a lot but then he would give me candy or ice cream. It would be bad for a few days and then I would forget for a while…until next time.

I didn't mind the dress-up playing. He would put fancy little dresses and shoes with little heels on me. Then he'd fix my hair and put makeup on my face. I'd prance around like a model on a stage or like someone in a beauty pageant. I had never heard of a beauty pageant but that's what he would tell me. "Let's play be a model today!" or "Let's play beauty pageant!"

I liked that part but it was the part that came after I didn't like.

During all the years I belonged to him, I was the only one he kept. All the others went away after a few hours, but not me. Never me. He said I was special.

Until one day when I wasn't.

I stare at him now. He looks so old. Old and stooped. His hair is gray and thin, his body is pale and frail. I've heard what they do to men like him in prison. I hope those things were done to him over and over for the past thirteen and a half years.

He stares at me, his lips smiling despite his current circumstances. I shouldn't have removed the gag. I'll put it back on before I go. Doesn't really matter. There's no one to hear him scream.

Would he scream? I don't know. He's up to something. I'm certain of that.

After all, like I said, he started this.

But I'm going to end it.

WEDNESDAY, MAY 2

DETECTIVE OLIVIA NEWHOUSE

I cradle my coffee. Can't get warm. Last night the temperature dropped to almost freezing. It's cold as hell this morning. Blackberry winter or one of those crazy little cold snaps that disturbs the spring warm-up each year. I can definitely do without an encore of last winter's unusually cold temps and all that extra snowfall.

I consider the names on the white board in our joint cubicle. Even a detective as senior as Walt doesn't get an office in the Criminal Investigations Division. Not enough offices. But we do get a larger cubicle, one big enough for our desks to sit face to face in the center of the small square. On one side we have a row of filing cabinets with anything else we need to store stacked on top; on the other side of our work area we have a white board and an extra chair for anyone we want to entertain with our scenarios and progress on a given case. The cramped digs aren't such a big deal. We spend most of our time in the field anyway.

"So we can't actually confirm that Sanchez is in Mexico?" I say this knowing my partner is well aware of our current dilemma. What I don't say is that the name is somehow familiar to me. It's a feeling I can't quite put my finger on. A knowing, some small fleeting flare of recognition that just won't be captured and assimilated. Sanchez doesn't have a criminal record, but somehow I've encountered him before. Or maybe it's only that I've run across someone with that same last name.

Walt shakes his head. "Both of his buddies, Lassiter and Watkins, are single with no significant others that I've been able to locate. I've called all three cell phones and left messages. Lassiter doesn't have any extended family that we know of so there's no one to reach out to for confirmation on his whereabouts. The other guy, Watkins, has a mother but she only knows that her son is on vacation in Mexico. She confirmed the trouble with cell service in the area where they're supposed to be."

I glance at my notes. "The three men drove in Sanchez's SUV so we can't easily corroborate travel."

"Nope." Walt scrubs at his chin. "I've put in a call to the feds to see if we can confirm whether or not their passports show they've left the country."

That could work. "Any ideas on when we'll hear back?"

He shrugs. "Soon I hope. You never know with the feds."

I can't argue that point. "Moving on." I scan the names on the board. "Considering the second blood type, we're still assuming Fanning is the vic and not some kid he nabbed off the street." The idea makes me sick. Walt and I don't talk about it too much but we both hope the scumbag is dead.

"Based on the report Reynolds faxed over this morning," Walt passes the single page to me for adding to the case board, "the blood found at the scene was maybe thirty-six hours old, give or take. I checked for any kids who went missing over the weekend. Got two but they were both found. Checked on missing adults as well. Only one came up and her body was discovered this morning. Took a bottle of sleeping pills and went to Centennial Park. A jogger noticed her body near the kids' playground. Downed the whole bottle of pills and went night-night for the last time. Her baby girl died in her sleep about a year ago. SIDS, according to the report. The husband says she couldn't learn to live with it."

I shake my head. "Damn."

That's another aspect of pregnancy I find terrifying. With my parents gone, I only have me to worry about. I'm an adult and totally responsible for the steps I take as well as the consequences of those steps. The idea of having a tiny human who depends on me is totally terrifying. If I make a mistake, he or she could pay the price. That's one hell of a scary thought. Like that poor dead woman, how do you live with the death of a child even if it isn't your fault?

Vaguely I wonder if the fact that I failed to include David in the scenario is an indication that

I'm not as committed to him as I should be...that perhaps I don't love him as deeply as I thought. Maybe I'm in love with the notion of being in love. Hitting thirty jarred my reality. Or maybe it was losing my father, the only family I had left, that pushed me over the edge. I don't like the prospect of being alone. And yet lately I seem to be pushing David away more often than pulling him toward me.

I assuage my guilt with the notion that it's hormones. Or maybe this whole moving in thing has pressed me into some emotional corner. Now that I'm impregnated, maybe I'm turning on him the way the female Black Widow will sometimes do her mate.

You are losing it, Liv.

Chalking up the ridiculous thought to yesterday's headache, I force my full attention back onto the case. "Since we don't have any other possibilities, for now, I guess we stick with the assumption that Fanning is the vic and move on to the next person of interest on our revenge list." I look to Walt. He's the senior detective. We'll do this whatever way he feels is the best route. The list seems the only logical one to me.

"I don't see a better strategy at this point," he admits. "Let's do it."

I toss my empty Starbucks cup and grab my jacket. Walt gets a call as we cross the bullpen. If we're lucky it'll be Reynolds with an update that will give us something more to go on.

When the call ends Walt doesn't say anything so I guess it wasn't Reynolds.

"The vet," he says in answer to my unspoken question as we push out into the brisk morning air.

"Vet?" My stride lengthens to keep up with my partner's long legs. I'm not exactly short, five seven, but Walt is six two and when he's distracted he hustles and forgets all about me. "Is Sandy sick?"

"Nah. It's time for her annual checkup and shots."

"Oh." I smile. "How's she doing?"

Sandy is Walt's yellow Lab. I love that darn dog. As big as she is, she's the most lovable creature. I've never had a dog of my own. Maybe it's time I did. Dogs can be good for kids, I think. I dismiss the notion. Way too early to go there.

"Sandy's doing great." We load into his black Tahoe. "What's the address?"

I rattle off the West side address of the elementary school where the next name on our list teaches and then review the few details we have. "Shelley Martin, thirty-two. At nine, she was one of Fanning's first known victims." I pull my seatbelt across my lap and snap it into place.

Walt exits the lot, heading across town. He drives for a while without speaking. Whenever he's quiet like this, something is up. Since he's generally an open book when it comes to what's going on in his life, it must be about me. Then again, there's a very good chance I'm being paranoid. Whatever the case, he has something besides the case and Sandy's vet appointment on his mind. He drums his thumbs on the steering wheel, glances repeatedly at me. Oh yeah, it's about me.

"What?" I finally ask, unable to bear the suspense for another second.

"You're feeling better this morning?"

I glance at Walt and wonder why he didn't ask me that question when I arrived at CID this morning, bearing both our favorite coffees from Starbucks. I distinctly recall asking him if he'd had another rough night. His eyes are bloodshot again, and his shirt is wrinkled—the latter is totally out of character for my partner. No matter that we've only been partners for two years, I've known Walt since I started at Metro. Everyone knows Walt. He's topnotch. Always on his A game. One of the most beloved detectives in all of Metro. Whenever there's a particularly sensitive situation that rouses emotion in the community the chief of police inherently wants Walt on the case. Nashville loves him. Maybe it's the cowboy boots and the extra heavy southern drawl or his plain-spokenness. Whatever it is, folks adore him. I was damn lucky to be chosen to fill the shoes left by his long-time partner when he retired.

All that said, I'm not ready to spill my guts about the pregnancy or my misgivings about the wedding just yet. I still haven't processed all the confusing emotions myself. *Right.* I'm kidding myself. What I really am not ready for is to confess that I may have jumped the gun on the decisions in my relationship with David. I made mistakes and he is the one who's going to be hurt.

I've really screwed up.

"I'm okay." I stare out the window, watch the passing landscape. I also have no desire to talk about how I lost the entire evening and night to that damned headache either. Total amnesia is never a good thing. On top of that, I certainly feel no urge to discuss how the hangover the pain left me with is determined to ruin my day. Instead, I decide to ignore it and hope it'll go away. Very mature.

"You were in pretty bad shape when I took you home. Is there something you can take when that happens?"

He slows for a left turn. "Sometimes the pills work, sometimes they don't." This is true, except even if I had the necessary medication I wouldn't be able to take the pills because I'm pregnant. Last night my only choice was to sleep it off.

"What about Preston? Did he take good care of you after I left?"

Preston. Walt has never called David by his given name. That alone says a lot about how my partner feels on the subject. All the more reason why I can't talk to him about how I'm feeling. "There was nothing David could do. The dark and the quiet are the only things that help."

Walt grunts. "Stella's sister had migraines. She said stress made them worse."

"You think I'm stressed, Walt?" I hide my smile. He and Stella had no children so he's kind of taken me under his wing. Treats me like a daughter sometimes. I can't exactly say I don't enjoy it. Since I lost my father, my friendship with Walt means more than ever. He's like family.

"Yep, I think that fancy fiancé of yours has you way too stressed." He parks in front of the elementary school. "I don't think you need him."

Although I've noticed he doesn't care too much for David, this is the first time he's come right out and said as much. Laughter bubbles out of me before I can stop it. "I know you don't like him, but to be fair you really don't know him."

Another grunt. "I know enough."

"Maybe you should come over for dinner again, spend a little more quality time with him."

He shuts the engine off and turns to me. "That won't change my mind, kid. Preston is arrogant and he thinks you should cater to his every whim. Breaking bread with him isn't going to change my mind."

"He is arrogant," I confess. "But he's never that way with me." Just impatient and obsessive about how things should be. If he asks me again about unpacking those damned boxes I might punch him. I keep that to myself. Violence is never pretty, particularly in a relationship.

"I guess," Walt offers, "if you're in love him and he's in love with you that's all that matters."

I reach for the door but Walt doesn't. He is evidently not finished yet.

"You love him, right?"

I sigh. "You asked me this before."

"That's not an answer."

I stare forward, thinking about the answer before I give it. Do I say what I should say or what I feel? "I want to be in love with him," I admit. "I love a lot of things about him—as long as we're not with his family."

"So you're not really *in* love with him." Walt stares at me, his wise gray eyes demanding an answer.

"I thought I was, but now I'm not so sure." Okay. There. I said it out loud. The ground didn't break open and swallow me. The world didn't capsize. The three-carat solitaire at home on my bedside table probably hasn't self-destructed. I don't wear the ring to work. Don't want to risk damaging it or losing it and, besides, the celebrity-sized-dazzler can be a distraction during an interview.

"It's not until you live with a person that you see who he or she really is," he warns.

I nod. "He was different before. Moving in has been eye opening for both of us, I'm sure. Everything has to be so perfect in his house. The unpacked boxes are just the tip of the iceberg. He's fanatical about how things look. I never noticed that until I moved under the same roof with him." I drop my head back against the seat. "He's driving me crazy. And I'm making him want to pull out his hair."

"Then you should give him the ring back and go home."

Until yesterday it would have been that simple. Now everything is complicated.

"I have to think about all this some more."

Walt winks at me. "You'll figure it out. You're way too smart to get yourself trapped in a relationship that doesn't include mutual respect."

I smile but inside I want to cry. There was a time when I thought I was smarter than this, that's for sure. The past few weeks it's as if my ability to think and act with reason and wisdom has deserted me. I've lost my footing and somehow I can't find it amid all the uncertainty and newness of suddenly being an adult orphan and a bride-to-be. Throw mother-to-be in the mix and I am totally sinking here.

Shelley Martin's principal is more than happy to send an assistant to sit with Martin's class while we speak to her. Walt assured the principal that Mrs. Martin was not in any sort of trouble, that we are hoping she might be able to help us with a case. Still, I doubt the curious principal will let it go. She will want answers. But whatever answers Martin gives are up to her.

We wait in the teacher's lounge. When Martin arrives she doesn't appear surprised to see us but she does seem nervous. She wears her black hair in a sleek twist. Her cream-colored trousers and blue shirt are modest. She wears only a simple gold band on her ring finger. She was Shelley Jones when the abduction occurred.

Walt explains that we're here to talk about Fanning. She flinches when he says the name. Then her cheeks redden and her lips tighten. Hearing his name makes her angry, justifiably so.

She says, "I heard on the news that he's missing."

"Mrs. Martin," I begin, "we need to ask you a few questions about him. Is that okay with you?"

She shifts her stern focus to me. "I loathe him. Pray every day that he will die as painfully as possible. He lured me into his car when I was nine years old. I'd gotten lost from my sister at the mall. He took me to the parking lot of an abandoned warehouse and raped me." She swallows hard. "He left me there naked, injured and terrified. I gave the police his description but they never found him. There was no evidence because he wore a condom and kept my clothes to ensure nothing from him or his car stuck to what I was wearing. It wasn't until many years later that he was caught. I came forward, testified against him. I hoped he would rot in prison but apparently that wasn't considered the sort of justice he deserved."

Her words are laced with hatred and bitterness. But who wouldn't feel that way?

"Mrs. Martin," Walt says gently, "we understand your feelings. You have every right to feel betrayed by how the legal system sometimes works. But we're here because it's our job to ensure no one else is harmed by the horrors Fanning carried out against you and so many others. With that in mind, would you tell us if you've seen him since he was released from prison?"

Her eyes round with fear. "I certainly have not. Do you have reason to believe he has been watching the people who testified against him?"

Her reaction is a logical one. No doubt every one of his victims has surely experienced that same thought.

"We don't," Walt admits.

Now for the hard question. My partner and I exchange a glance and I take the lead. "Ma'am, can you tell us where you were on Sunday and Monday?"

The anger vanishes from her face and shock takes its place. I brace for the blast of outrage.

"Are you suggesting I had something to do with his disappearance?"

"No, ma'am," I assure her. "We're only trying to determine who may have seen him or heard from him. You may be able to help us figure out what happened."

Fury twists Martin's lips for another moment before she regains her composure. "My family had a big breakfast at home Sunday morning and then I took my twin daughters shopping. Sunday was their birthday. The girls, my husband and I arrived home about nine that evening and I didn't leave again until I came to school the next morning. I picked up my girls after school on Monday and went home. My family can confirm I was home all night both Sunday and Monday."

We already confirmed with the principal that Martin was at school all day on Monday. "Thank you," I say. "We appreciate your cooperation."

She shakes her head, fury still radiating from her. "How dare you come to me—interrupt my day at school—with such a ludicrous question." She jams her thumb into her chest. "*I* am the victim."

Walt and I share another look. He says, "Mrs. Martin, we haven't released to the public what I'm about to tell you. We would appreciate it if you don't share this part with anyone."

Her anger drains away instantly as fear of the unknown creeps in and takes its place. "You have my word."

"The other person involved with whatever happened to Fanning was injured. We found a second blood type at the scene. Our goal with these questions is to figure out if someone else was hurt by Fanning the night he disappeared. If that's the case, we may have someone out there in need of our help and we don't even know it."

"You're saying he may have taken another victim?" The abject horror on her face is palpable.

"We can't say anything for sure," I counter.

"This is why," Walt goes on, "it's extremely important that we ask these hard questions of anyone who is connected in any way to Fanning. For all we know, you may have driven by his place—accidentally or not—and noticed someone who might be relevant to whatever happened there."

She shakes her head. "I have no idea where he lives. I saw on the news that he'd been released and I tried not to think of him again. Of course it was impossible. Before the trial I was just an anonymous little girl he picked up at the mall and did bad things to. My name was never released in the news. But then, at the trial, I had to face him. He learned my name, where my parents and sister lived. I won't lie, I've been looking over my shoulder since the day he was released."

"That's completely understandable," I say. Deep in my skull the ache begins and I refuse to acknowledge it. I have never had a migraine so many times in one week. This is really wrong.

We apologize again for disturbing her day and leave the school.

"Somehow I don't think we're going to find out what happened to that bastard through his victims."

I agree with Walt. But we have to confirm that theory. We can't skip any steps. This is way too important. Someone's life could depend on what we do. And I damn sure don't mean Fanning's.

When we stop for lunch I check in with my doctor's office to see if I can manage an appointment later today. They have a cancellation at two. I glance at the clock on the wall of Taco Mama's. It's one now. I take the appointment. I need to know what's going on with my head.

When Walt returns from the men's room I say, "I need to pick up my car. My doctor can see me at two. Maybe she can give me something to help with these migraines."

"I'll take you," he announces. "I can make some phone calls while I wait."

I want to argue, but I have no desire to beat my head against that particular brick wall. Walt is as stubborn as he is good at being a detective and a friend.

After peeing in a cup and having blood drawn, I sit on the edge of the exam table and wait impatiently while Dr. Raeford goes through the findings listed in my chart. I told her about the pregnancy tests and about the headaches. About the move. She already knew my father died and that I'd gotten engaged. My annual exam was in March and all was good. How did so much change since then?

Hopefully she can give me some clue as to why the headaches are back with such a vengeance. I really can't afford to be taking any time off work right now. Walt needs me. And the idea of spending twenty-four/seven in David's house is more than I can stomach.

The thought stops me. Part of me feels as if I'm making him the bad guy in all this, but it's more than that. I can't explain these new and intense feelings. Every instinct I possess is sounding an alarm that something bad is coming and I can't stop it. Whatever it is, it somehow involves my relationship with David. The urge to run is strong but I feel *trapped* by the promises I've made. Cold feet? Who the hell knows, but this fear of needing to escape is the best way I know to explain it. I have no idea how I'm going to find my way out of this corner.

Bottom line, running away isn't an option. Not that I've ever run from anything.

"Well, everything I can see here looks normal." Dr. Raeford smiles at me. "Of course some of the tests will take a few days. You are, indeed, pregnant. Based on your last period I'd say five or six weeks. Considering the fact that your last period was so light, there's a possibility you could be nine or ten. We'll schedule an ultrasound for your next appointment to get a better handle on where you are."

Oh God. This is real.

Smiling just a little at the fear on my face, she goes on, "The wacky hormones you're experiencing right now are quite possibly a major contributor to the headaches. The good news is those hormones usually level out in the second trimester. I suspect having recently lost your father, getting engaged and moving in with your fiancé have your stress level off the charts." She glances at my file again. "Your blood pressure is a little high but that might just be related to the lack of sleep or the headaches or maybe just because you're nervous or worried. Even tough-as-nails cops like you can get a little nervous and worried sometimes."

I nod. Definitely nervous and worried. I am not ready for this. But it's real and I have to get that way fast. These issues with David have to be worked out. This child will need both of us.

She scans my file. "You said this is your first pregnancy?"

I nod again, realize she's still perusing the file and say, "Yes."

She makes some notes on my chart.

"About the headaches, is there anything I can take to help?" I steady my voice and keep going. "They're interfering with work and it's just not a good time for me to be sick. My partner and I are in the middle of this big case." I don't say as much but that's not actually unusual. We're always on a case and with Walt as a partner they're generally the most difficult and high profile ones.

Another smile from the doctor. "Is there ever a good time to be sick?"

I shrug. "True."

She picks up a prescription pad and starts filling in the blanks. "Sadly, there isn't anything beyond Tylenol that I would recommend you take. You've had migraines before, you know the triggers. Try to avoid them. Relax as much as you can. That will help." She removes the top page from the pad and passes it to me.

I stare at the illegible words. It's a good thing cops don't write the way doctors do.

"For now," she goes on, "you need to get started with prenatal vitamins. I'll let you know if there's anything else you should be taking once we have your blood work back. But based on your physical just two months ago, I'd say the headaches are nothing more than stress and hormones. Exercise and meditation are good sources of stress relief during pregnancy.

Take long walks in the evenings. Lie down with some hot tea and relax. Put everything else on hold for now. Those are simple things you can do to help."

Except nothing is simple right now. Not in my world.

DETECTIVE WALTER DUNCAN

"That was fast." I open the lobby door for Liv and follow her out of the doctor's office. I'm hoping the doc was able to give her something that will keep the headaches at bay until her life calms down.

Now that's rich. Since when does a cop's life ever calm down?

When Liv walks straight to the bank of elevators and presses the call button without a word, I trudge after her. I suppose she'll tell me what she wants to tell me in her own time. We've worked together for two years. She's seen the worst of me and so far she's been open and honest about herself, as have I.

Until recently anyway.

I can't exactly fault her for holding things close to the vest when I'm keeping a whopper of a secret myself. I don't like being that man and the guilt is weighing on me. Stella always said the reason she loved me so much was because I was a good man, an honest man.

I need to get back to being that man.

When the elevator doors close with us inside, she finally speaks. "She's pretty sure it's not a brain tumor."

Her lips quirk and I smile. "That's always good."

"She did some blood work. Mostly she thinks it's the stress."

"Ah ha!" I grin and keep the *I told you so* to myself.

"Yeah, yeah." She leans against the back wall. "I need more sleep and less upset in my life. But I'm a cop and I don't really see how that's possible."

"Speaking of upset," I say, "Reynolds finished his preliminary work up on the evidence collected from the Fanning scene. Clean as a whistle for the most part. Fanning's prints were the only ones he could identify. Whoever else was involved, he or she wasn't in the database or was extremely careful. Didn't leave anything behind except the blood on that hand towel and, for all we know, it may've already been there. Reynolds said there's still some trace evidence to go through but he's not expecting any game changers."

"This is what television dramas like CSI give us," she gripes, "evidence free crime scenes."

She rubs at her forehead and my gut clenches. "Did your doc give you anything for the headaches?"

She shakes her head. "For now, she wants to hold off. See what's going on with the blood work."

"Makes sense, I guess." I sure as hell hate for Liv to suffer the way she did yesterday. It was painful just watching.

She glances at the screen on her phone. "We still have time to try and catch Dana Reeves at her office."

The elevator bumps to a stop. "I can handle the next interview if you want to call it a day."

She glares at me before stepping off the car. "No way, this is my case, too."

"Yes, ma'am."

We load up and head to the south side. Dana Reeves is a CPA with her own shop off Powell Avenue in Woodbine. Reeves was eleven when she was picked up by Fanning twenty-two years ago. According to what we could dig up she never married and has no children. She lives in the same apartment she moved into after college. Never been arrested. No traffic violations. The only hit we got on her name was the registrations for three dogs. I hope all three are big, badass guard dogs. Anyone who's been violated, particularly in such a vile way, should get a big old mean dog. My Sandy is far from a badass but, if necessary, she would go down trying to protect me.

Liv studies the file for most of the trip. Usually she talks about what she's reading, bounces thoughts off me. Not today. Today she's oddly quiet. For the most part, she's been that way all week. I wonder again if the doctor said more than she's telling.

"Dana was the only girl from Belle Meade who ended up a victim of Fanning," I say, in hopes of nudging her into the conversation.

Liv closes the file and stares straight ahead. "Her parents still live in Belle Meade. So do her two brothers. But she never went back after she left home for college. If her address is any indication, she lives frugally."

"The Pontiac registered to her is nearly as old as she is." Nothing wrong with that. I hung on to my first car until I was thirty, and it was well on its way to that milestone, too. "You're right, she's either not making a whole lot of money or she chooses to be tight with what she does make."

"It's possible she and her parents had a falling out," Liv offers.

"Or maybe she likes to travel and spends all her money on vacations?" I regret that Stella and I didn't travel more. We always put off those plans. Maybe next year, I'd say. She would agree, though I suspected she just went along with whatever I thought. The job always took priority and the next thing we knew it was too late.

"She has no kids, no husband," Liv remarks, sounding more like herself now.

"She owns her own business," I add.

That out-of-character silence returns; hangs in the air as I take the turn for Powell Avenue. I glance at Liv but she's staring out the window.

"I find it strange there was no true pattern to Fanning's choice in victims. At least not one the investigation discovered all those years ago," I say as I slow for a crosswalk. "The age range was unusually broad. Hair and eye color didn't seem to matter." I shrug. "No order to the when or the where he chose to strike. No set MO for how he made the abduction or for what happened after. Well, other than the fact that all his victims were left alive—as far as we know anyway."

I frown, thinking back to the rabid news coverage of the trial. "Even after he was sentenced, he refused to talk about what drove him, what made him do the things he did. Most of them talk eventually. But not Fanning. He never said a word."

More of that heavy silence crowds in as soon as I stop talking. I glance at Liv to make sure she's still awake.

"He chose what he wanted in the moment," she says, her voice distant as if she's remembering rather than theorizing. "They were all beautiful to him."

I nod slowly. "Did you read that somewhere in the file?"

She jerks her head toward me, blinks as if she'd just realized I was in the car with her. "I'm sorry, what did you say?"

"What you said about him thinking they were all beautiful, did you read that in the file somewhere?" I don't remember seeing it.

"I must have."

I brake for the traffic signal, my blinker on for the final turn. A frown lines her face as if she's trying to recall where she read the conclusion. "This would be a lot easier if I'd worked the case," I admit, "but I was in the hospital having my appendix removed. Stach and Quinn caught the case."

"Detective Quinn," she says. "Maybe I read something to that effect in his notes."

"Maybe so," I agree, though I'm reasonably confident I reviewed all his notes, too. I could have read over that particular comment. After a while it all blurs together.

Quinn died five years ago, shot at a domestic violence scene. Left a wife and three grown kids behind. I wonder sometimes if Stella had been able to have children, if we would have filled the empty rooms of our home. We talked about adopting but the timing never seemed to be right and then we were old.

Where the hell did the years go?

Reeves Accounting is open. There's no one waiting in the lobby but the receptionist informs us that Ms. Reeves has a client with her and that it might be a while. I tell her we'll wait.

Liv picks up a magazine and thumbs absently through it. She pretends to look at the pictures but I know she's not. She's soaking up the vibe of the place. The fresh paint on the walls, the stacks of current magazines on the tables. Newly upholstered chairs; the industrial style tile polished to a high sheen on the floor. Even the receptionist's desk looks shiny and new. A jungle of plants stand in front of the big plate glass window. The neighborhood might be low rent, but the suite of offices is well done and immaculately maintained.

Twenty minutes later the door opens and the client exits. The receptionist goes into her boss's office for a moment and then returns, leaving the door open.

"Ms. Reeves will see you now."

"Thanks." I give her a nod and follow Liv into the plush office.

The office is carpeted and decked out. Expensive drapes. High-end upholstered wingbacks. The woman, Dana Reeves, is dressed professionally in a gray suit and pink blouse. Her dark hair is cut short. She's gained a considerable amount of weight since she renewed her license four years ago.

"I'm Detective Newhouse," Liv says, "this is my partner, Detective Duncan. We'd like to ask you a few questions."

Reeves gestures to the chairs in front of her desk. "I'm always happy to help Metro. Please, make yourselves at home. Would you like water or a coffee?"

We both decline.

"Is this about the break-in next door?"

Liv and I exchange a look. I say, "No, ma'am, we're not here about the break-in."

Some cops don't like to do cold interviews unless absolutely necessary. Personally I've decided that folks are far more forthcoming with straight answers if they haven't had time to prepare. No matter if they're completely innocent, they're only human and most people worry about anything they say making them look guilty. It's better not to give them the opportunity to overanalyze.

Reeves nods slowly, confusion beginning to show on her face.

"Ma'am," Liv kicks off the interview, "we're here about Joseph Fanning."

The CPA's eyes flare. "I see."

Her voice is cool, low and her expression closes instantly.

"I'm sure you're aware," I explain, "he was released last month."

She nods. "I was upset at first but I've come to terms with the fact that he paid the debt the court required of him, fair or not."

"He hasn't contacted you or showed up at your home or business?" Liv asks.

Fear rounds the older woman's eyes. "No. Has he done that to someone else? Another of his victims?"

"Not that we know of," I assure her. "But there was an incident at his place of residence on Sunday or Monday and he's missing. We're worried that he may have someone else with him."

"Sweet Jesus." She presses a hand to her chest. "You people should never have let him off so easy with that damned plea deal! What the hell were you thinking? Now he may have hurt someone else?" She shakes her head. "I can't believe this is happening."

Now for the hard part. Before I can ask, Liv does, "Ms. Reeves, can you tell us where you were between Sunday morning and Monday afternoon?"

Outrage rushes up her neck and spreads across her plump cheeks, leaving a swath of red. "Why on earth would you ask me such a question?" Her gaze narrows. "Are you accusing me of something?"

"We are not, Ms. Reeves," I say firmly. "We are simply following up with all his victims to determine if he or anyone else involved with him has made any sort of contact with you, particularly on Sunday or Monday of this week."

The red drains from her face and she visibly gathers her composure. "I have not seen or heard from him or anyone related to him. I would have called the police if I had. As for my whereabouts, on Sunday I was at church until noon and then I went to have lunch with my family. My parents can confirm I was there until around four. After that I went home. I didn't leave my apartment again until I came to work on Monday morning."

"Can any of your neighbors confirm you were home?" Liv asks. "Maybe you walked your dogs?"

"My wife can confirm I was home. She was at home with me."

I definitely didn't find a marriage license. "May we have her name and a way to contact her?"

"Of course." Reeves jots down a name and number on the back of one of her business cards and passes it to me.

"Thank you, Ms. Reeves," Liv says as she pushes up from her chair. "Please let us know if you hear from Fanning or anyone involved in any way with him."

I pass the woman one of my business cards. She stares at it and nods.

We leave. The receptionist watches until we're out the door.

Once we're in the Tahoe, I start the engine and see the receptionist locking the door and turning the open sign to closed.

"I guess we ruined her afternoon." Liv fastens her seatbelt.

"Guess so." I reach for the gearshift and a coughing jag hits me. It takes me half a damned minute to get the hacking under control.

Liv passes me her water bottle. "Damn, Walt. You need to get that cough checked out."

I down some water and grunt. My chest feels as if I just hawked up a lung. "Allergies," I lie.

Liv reaches for the card from Reeves that I dropped when the coughing started.

"Well, that's interesting."

I clear my throat as I back out of the parking slot. "What?"

"Based on the name Reeves gave us, her wife is another one of Fanning's victims."

DETECTIVE OLIVIA NEWHOUSE

The house is quiet when I arrive. I breathe a little easier as I close the front door and disable the alarm. I couldn't find my garage door opener so I had to leave my Subaru out front. Something else he won't like.

It's after seven. I can't believe he's not home.

I flip on the light and lean against the closed door. The crystal chandelier sends sparkles over the shiny marble floor and along the polished wood bannister that leads up to the second floor landing.

How can I possibly ever feel like this is home? I should have realized this life was a pipedream—something meant for a different kind of woman. One who adores the social life and plans months in advance to ensure no one misses a single one of her parties.

I can't be that person.

My boxes. Eight large moving boxes picked up from a U-Haul store close to the farm sit to the right of the front door, near the grand entrance to the dining room. There are dozens more of these same boxes at the farm—at the only home I've ever known, the only place I've ever felt comfortable— waiting to be filled. At the house I'm supposed to be packing up to sell. How do you pack up a lifetime of living? Not just my life but the lives of my parents? My father bought the farm right after I was born. He and Mom decided they didn't want their only child growing up in the city. I never attended public school. I was homeschooled until I went to college and even then I lived at home.

I push away from the door and approach the boxes. I packed each one myself. Brought them here jammed into Walt's Tahoe and in my Subaru. David was pleased at first. Happy to see me taking steps toward our future, he'd professed.

I wonder now if that's what I was doing? Or was I just trying to keep him happy? To keep him off my back? Either way, I promised him I would deal with the boxes. Since they're well taped I'll need a box cutter. I blink, inventory my level of exhaustion. Maybe not tonight, I decide. Tonight I'm too tired.

The distant throb in my skull has not evolved into another headache and for that I am extremely grateful. But I know from experience my luck won't last. I can't remember the last time I had clusters of migraines like this. The headaches usually came one at a time with weeks in between. This is new and agonizing territory.

But then I've never been pregnant before. Never been engaged or grieving the loss of the last of my family.

Slowly I climb the stairs. A long hot shower will help, I hope. I would really love a couple of beers but that's not an option.

Shit. I forgot to pick up the prenatal vitamins.

I stall on the landing. So, I guess I'm really doing this?

Of course I am. I was raised Catholic. But am I capable of being a mother?

Somehow my feet continue moving toward the bedroom. As always the bed is made even though I crawled out of the tangle of linens without looking back. The duvet is plump and blinding white, made of the finest cottons and filled with lush down. If I fell onto it now I would sink into its lavish depths. Pillows, their white cases banded with gold, are arranged three deep against the rich wood headboard. Beneath all that soft white are luxury sheets. Sleeping in this bed is like staying in a five-star hotel.

There are two housekeepers who come in everyday. My clothes—generally left in a wad in the hamper—are always laundered and hung in the closet. I walk through the room and into the bathroom, strip off my clothes and climb into the shower. There is no waiting for the water to get hot; it's instantaneous.

I stand beneath the spray and the question haunts me again. Am I capable of being a mother?

Drugs have never been a part of my life. I drink too much beer sometimes, but not often. Don't smoke. Though I attended church with my parents growing up, I haven't been in years. Occasionally I swear like the proverbial sailor and am not known for my infinite patience. My housekeeping skills leave something to be desired. But I do eat reasonably healthy foods when I take the time to eat.

I stare at my flat belly. I should be eating regularly now.

However shocking and unexpected this reality, I have an obligation to do the right thing for me and for the baby.

Twenty minutes later with my hair dried and my favorite t-shirt and lounge pants on, I head downstairs to do something about dinner. I glance at the clock. Almost eight. Where is David?

I have to admit I'm enjoying the peace without him—how sad is that?

The sixty-inch built-in fridge is filled with offerings. Leftover pot roast looks good. I guess David had pot roast last night while I was lost to the migraine. That's the other thing about living here. A cook comes most afternoons and prepares dinner, unless we're scheduled to go out.

I place the clear plastic container on the counter and go still. If there is no dinner prepared for tonight, then there was an engagement on the calendar.

"Oh shit."

I drag out my cell, only then noting the four unopened text messages from David. One came late this afternoon. Don't forget we have dinner with the family tonight. All the moisture evaporates from my throat. The next one came at five. I'm sure you're in the middle of something

but don't forget about tonight. There is another of a similar nature at five-thirty. The one at six is different. Never mind. I've told Mother you're working late.

My appetite vanishes in a cloud of frustration and regret. I check my phone's calendar. Yep. The dinner was there. How the hell did I forget? And why the hell hadn't he called me? It's easy to ignore text messages. Usually I don't ignore that many but after seeing the doctor I was a little shell shocked. Taking the home pregnancy tests was one thing but having my doctor tell me that I'm pregnant and all the things I should be doing was truly life altering.

I could tell David and all would be forgiven in a burst of astonishment and happiness and celebratory tears. He is the type of man who isn't afraid to show his emotions. I'm the one who keeps things hidden. My father called it a self-protective mechanism.

No one can use against you what he doesn't know.

I force myself to eat. The television on the kitchen counter is always on but the sound is muted. Joseph Fanning's face flashes on the screen and I look away. A child could go missing and he or she wouldn't warrant the density of coverage focused on this disgusting pedophile. I banish the frustration that comes with the thought and finish off my dinner. If the media coverage helps us find the scumbag, then I should be glad for it.

A quick rinse of my bowl and I tuck it into the dishwasher. I should leave a note telling the cook, whose name I don't even know, how much I enjoyed the pot roast. I saw her once when she was leaving for the day and I was arriving. She reminded me of my mother. Red hair pulled back into a neat twist. Petite. She looked to be about the age my mother would be if she were still alive.

I stare at my reflection in the window over the sink, the blond hair, the blue eyes. I didn't get my mother's red hair or my father's brown or their dark chocolate colored eyes. But the sprinkling of freckles across the bridge of my nose is exactly as my mother's was. My father swore I had his mind and I probably do. As a psychiatrist, his life's work was about analyzing people. I suppose as a cop my work, to some degree, is as well. He and I thought very much alike, that's true. Looking back, I find the idea funny because most of my early years were spent primarily with my mother. She was my mom, my schoolteacher, my riding instructor.

As a young woman, Corrine Newhouse was an award-winning equestrian. Though I competed in my share of local shows early on, they never wanted that notoriety for me. They kept me close, protected me from the world until I was too old to be sheltered any longer. As much as they shielded me, they also prepared me. I had the best private self-defense classes. Knew how to shoot a weapon, how to escape trouble, all before my first day as a freshman at college.

Thinking back on what my father called the MacGyver classes, I smile. He taught me how to take the simplest objects and utilize them as tools for protecting myself and for escaping captivity.

The walls of any prison are only as impenetrable as you allow them to be. Escape is always possible, even if only in your mind.

I never mentioned these lessons to my college friends since none of them ever mentioned having been taught such things. My dad took readiness to the next level. He was one of a kind.

My phone vibrates against the granite countertop. Easy to hear in the silent kitchen. I tell myself that if I'd had a moment of silence this afternoon I would have realized David's texts were waiting.

I pick up my cell, hope it's him wanting to know if I ever made it home. It would be far easier to apologize via text than face to face.

Not David. *Walt.*

A photo of Dana Reeves and Janie Hyatt appears on the screen. The photo appears several years old. The two women look like teenagers. Reeves has longer hair and is much slimmer.

Where'd you get this?

I send the text.

Facebook. LOL. Apparently the two have been together since high school.

Nashville is a large city. It's not impossible that two of Fanning's victims just happened to end up together in high school but it seems a little unexpected considering the two women had not lived in the same neighborhood.

Interesting, I type back.

Here I am knocking around memory lane and Walt has been working. I pull up the Facebook app and search for Reeves and Hyatt. The two went to college together. Hyatt is a nurse at Vanderbilt. On both pages I notice several photos of them at a cabin. Definitely not the dumpy south side apartment where Reeves lives.

Any ideas about this cabin? I send the question to Walt.

Got a friend looking through property records at this very moment.

That's the thing about being part of Metro for as long as Walt has. He knows everyone. Has serious contacts all over. I hope he introduces me to even half of them before he retires.

Another text appears on my screen.

Bingo. Hyatt inherited a cabin and ten acres way out in the middle of nowhere in Hendersonville. Road trip tomorrow.

Images of Fanning being held by one or more of his victims flash in my head. I close my eyes against the pain that follows. Damn it. Not tonight. Tonight I need to sleep. Tonight I need to make up for my negligence toward David.

I send Walt a thumbs-up and force myself to finish off the glass of milk I'd poured. I give myself a mental pat on the back for eating a decent meal for a change and decide maybe I will tear into those boxes. I search the cabinet drawers for a knife since I have no idea where a box cutter would be.

Knife in hand, I wander to the entry hall and size up the stack. Maybe if I at least get started on one and actually take a few items upstairs David won't be so mad when he comes home.

Yeah, right.

He will be pissed. Twice a month his entire family gets together for dinner. The two brothers, the sister, their spouses and offspring descend upon the family home and catch up over the meal prepared by the family's private chef. David's parents have a full-time chef, two housekeepers and two gardeners. Oh yeah, David has basically the same staff only the cook is part-time and maybe not an actual chef.

These are things I should be grateful for and somehow I can only see the waste and self-importance of living so large. Why did I not notice this before? Giving myself grace, until I moved in we spent more time at the farm or at some restaurant downtown than at his house. Still, I should have done a better job of sizing up the situation the first time I went to dinner at his parents' palatial home.

Is this my way of finding a reason to break up? This sudden need to pick apart every aspect of David's lifestyle? Am I subconsciously looking for a way out?

Pushing the worries aside I reach for a box, prepared to slice through the tape holding the flaps. But the flaps are already loose on this one. When did I do that?

The security system chimes and announces: *Garage door open.*

David's home.

I lay the knife aside and reach for the box. None of them are labeled so I have no clue what's inside. I've barely pulled one flap open when he appears in the dining room, jacket slung over his shoulder.

"You forgot."

"Sorry. I don't know how I did. It was on my calendar." I shake my head, infusing as much contrition as possible into my voice. I really am sorry. I don't want to embarrass him in front of his family and I'm certain my inability to show up for their bimonthly dinners is very awkward for him. "My only excuse is that it has been a crazy week."

"I sent you several texts."

He keeps his voice low and even, but I hear the anger simmering beneath all that control. He's seriously pissed. I guess I don't blame him.

"I didn't see them until I got home." I reach for another of the flaps.

"What held you up?" He moves closer now, the edge in his voice more prominent, his face a mask made of stone.

"We're interviewing Fanning's victims. We have no choice but to work with their schedules. When I'm in an interview, I have no choice but to ignore my phone."

"Oh yeah." He glances upward in obvious frustration and then shakes his head. "Interviewing potential suspects is far more important than dinner with my family."

I drop my hands from the box and take a breath. I am not going to fight with him. Clearly, that's what he wants. "Not suspects, persons of interest and, for the record, I'm a cop," I remind him. "It's my job. We have possibly two missing persons. One or both may be gravely injured or dead. Time is our enemy."

"He's a pedophile." The words come out a low roar. "Who gives a damn if someone dragged him off somewhere to torture and murder him? He deserves it."

I can't say that I don't feel the same way, except that I can't allow my personal feelings to interfere with my work. "It's my job. Whatever he is, the law protects him as much as it does anyone else."

He stares at me. I'm not sure whether it's disbelief or defeat on his face. Whatever it is, he is far from finished.

"Why did you sleep in the guest room last night?"

I frown, then realize he couldn't know the answer. "I had the worst migraine of my life yesterday. I had to leave work and close myself up in a dark room. It was awful."

Something like sympathy flashes across his face but it doesn't last. "I'm sorry to hear that." He shrugs. "Of course, I wouldn't know because we never talk anymore." His voice rises with each word.

I close my eyes and grab tighter onto my own self-control. I refuse to allow this to turn into a war. "I told you the other day that I suffered horrible migraines as a teenager." I open my eyes and look directly into his. "I haven't had one for a very long time. The reason I didn't hear your first text was because I was at the doctor's office trying to figure out why the hell they're back." Like his, my voice rises despite my best efforts to keep it steady. I hesitate, calm myself. "The appointment put us behind so we had no choice but to work late."

"We?" He shakes his head. "You and Walt, right?"

I take a deep breath, hoping it will slow the pounding in my chest. "He is my partner."

"I don't see why you don't marry him. After all, the two of you are always together. He knows all your secrets. Takes you to the doctor. I saw the way he took care of you at your father's funeral. You are more than partners, Olivia. I'd have to be blind not to have seen it."

That part is true. Walt and I are more than partners. We are friends. Good friends. From the day we became partners he has been a friend and mentor to me. "Walt didn't ask me to marry him," I say. "You did and I said yes."

My words take the fire out of him, at least for a moment.

"Then why doesn't it feel like you want to be with me?"

I hold my breath. Now would be the time to tell him about the baby. And it is a baby. Not just a pregnancy. There's another human growing inside me. One David and I created together.

I can't. Not yet. He will take complete control of my life then. He's already crowding me to the point I feel as if I can't breathe.

"I'm sorry about missing dinner with your family. I truly am," I say carefully. "I'm even sorrier that you're having doubts about our relationship. Relationships go through stages, David. It's normal for one or both of us to have the occasional doubt or misgiving."

He scoffs. "Do not try psychoanalyzing me or our relationship, Olivia. I will not stand for it."

"My father was the shrink, not me."

"Not just any shrink," he reminds me. "The top shrink in the city. You learned from the best and I am tired of feeling as though you're manipulating our relationship with this adept ability you have to make me the bad guy in whatever happens."

I mentally grasp for the last threads of my composure. "You're the one who rushed the issue of marriage," I remind him. I am beyond pissed now. However hard I try, there is no holding back. "You refused to let it go until I agreed to move in and now you want to complain about my work and even the fact that I had a headache last night and had to escape into the darkness for relief." I shout the last and I hate, hate, hate losing control to this extent.

Control is everything.

My father's voice echoes in my ears.

The only person who can take it from you is you, Olivia. Do not look back, only forward. What happened in the past is irrelevant. All that matters is what happens now.

"I see." David's head hangs as if he cannot bear to look at me.

"I'm really, really sorry." The words are stiff but I say them anyway. "I will call your mother in the morning and apologize. I will make sure I check my phone more frequently in the future so I don't miss your texts. I let you down and I will do all in my power not to let it happen again."

His gaze meets mine and in that instant, staring into his beautiful eyes, I see the man who stole my heart. He is, under normal circumstances, kind and considerate. He will be a good father and a good husband—as soon as he learns that he cannot keep me on a leash when it comes to my work. I want very much to find a way to work this out. To take us back to the way things were before…whatever changed.

"Thank you." He moves closer to me. "Forget about the boxes for tonight. Let's go upstairs." He searches my face. "As long as you're feeling up to it."

Rather than answer I kiss him. I kiss him until we both lose our breath.

He takes me in his arms and carries me upstairs.

When all else fails, distract. The most vulnerable prey can outwit a predator with the right distraction.

Another piece of handy advice the man who raised me instilled.

DETECTIVE WALTER DUNCAN

It's the holes—the ones that go unrecognized for a little too long that cause the most trouble—in the best-laid plans.

I sit on the back porch steps, my loyal companion at my side. We both stare out across the lawn for as far as the light will reach through the darkness. I think of Stella's roses and how inept and pathetic I've proven at trying to keep them healthy and blooming. My Stella was a natural with plants. Our yard, front and back, was always a standout in the neighborhood.

Until Stella suddenly got sick, the yard was her domain. Of course, I navigated the lawnmower around the property on Saturdays, kept the grass trimmings up, but the rest was her territory and she had shooed me out of her flowerbeds more than once. She would be horrified if she could see the overgrown mess they have become. I'm glad it's dark and I don't have to look at them.

Neither she nor I ever considered the possibility that I needed to learn how to take care of those things. Never seemed necessary. She was here. Healthy, years younger than me. I was the cop, the smoker until a mere five years ago. If anyone was going to end up dead a little early in the game, it was me.

Except we'd been wrong.

In an effort to go into this final rush toward the finish line with both eyes open and all potential gaps in the strategy covered, I have been carefully organizing and planning my demise. It's inevitable. Nothing I can do to stop it. No use lying to myself. Pretending was never my strong suit unless it was necessary to prompt a suspect to talk. I can be a pretty good actor when the occasion calls for it.

But in all my elaborate planning and thorough consideration I forgot the most important thing in my life, besides Liv and my work—Sandy. At eighty-five pounds and taller than me when she stands on her hind legs, my yellow lab should be hard to forget. And yet, I left her completely out of the scenario until that call from the vet.

I've made arrangements at the funeral home to be buried next to my wife without the bother of a funeral. I told the funeral director to do what he had to do and plant me, no frills, no fuss. My house, everything inside it and the SUV I bequeathed to Stella's favorite charity. She and I donated her car to the same charity before she closed her eyes for the last time. I considered leaving my savings and insurance money to Liv, but she doesn't need it. She would be the first to say her parents left her far more than she will ever need. So I decided to assign it to my favorite charity—the families of wounded and fallen officers. My fellow officers are the only real family I have. Like Liv, I was an only child. Parents are long gone. I was never close to the few distant cousins I met as a kid.

I've been so thorough with all the necessary final arrangements. How in the world did I allow anything—especially something as important as my sweet Sandy—to fall through the cracks in my preparations?

Maybe because I didn't want to face the fact that leaving a dog behind is a true dilemma, not like the money or the material possessions. I'm reasonably sure Liv would take her in a heartbeat but I don't know how the knucklehead would feel about it. I shouldn't care but if she's going to marry the man, I need to try and respect that. Maybe I could bring up the subject of pets with her and get a feel for Preston's take on such things.

"Don't worry, girl." I rub Sandy's back and pull her against me. "I'll make sure you have a good home."

Sandy turned ten this year. Never been sick a day in her life. Her last annual checkup was all good, I expect the upcoming one will be as well. She's had all her shots. Even though she eats like a horse, she's worth the cost of kibbles because she's a damn good watchdog. A damn good companion. Stella put a big bow on her and tucked her into a box for my fiftieth birthday. I remember thinking what the hell am I going to do with a dog. I'm not home nearly as much as I should be. How will I take care of a dog? What on earth had she been thinking?

It didn't take long to figure out the dog was more for Stella than for me. She was lonely and didn't want to hurt my feelings by telling me. So she got a dog. By the end of year one we were down a few pairs of shoes, but both of us were in love with the animal. I toss the tennis ball Sandy loves to chase and wait for her to bring it back to me, then I throw it again. At least one of us will get some exercise today.

A blast of heavy air puffs out of me and I wonder how many weeks I have left before the pain becomes unbearable. Since Stella started the treatments within two weeks of her diagnosis, she was sick as hell by now. Other than the coughing jags that are becoming more and more frequent, I haven't had too much trouble. I have the pain meds just in case. As the doctor said, there's no use in a dying man suffering.

But I will. That, too, is inevitable. The job comes first, at least as long as I'm standing.

Liv looked like hell again today. I don't like that those migraines are taking her down so low. In the two years we've worked so closely together I've never known her to look anything but healthy and vibrant. She seems almost withdrawn lately. Distracted and fatigued. The big ass bags under her eyes underscored by the dark circles have me worried. But she went to the doc. I was there in the waiting room. Her doctor didn't seem overly concerned. These days I'm not sure if that is a good thing or not. Sometimes I think they just run us through like scanning groceries at the supermarket checkout. If you're turned the wrong way they might not pick up on the real problem. It's all scary as hell and it feels like nothing more than the luck of the draw.

The good news is, Liv is smart. And she's strong. No matter that she's a little off her game right now, she'll pull it together. That's something else I know about her.

"Come on, Sandy." I stand, stretch my back and lead the way into the house.

I fill her water bowl and move to the fridge to scrounge around for a late snack. Thirty-five years I came home to a hot meal prepared from scratch, unless we went out which was rare. I'm spoiled and mostly inept in the kitchen. I round up cheese and crackers and snag a beer.

With my arm full of goodies, I drop into a chair at the table. My working case file lies open on the table. Photos of the known victims of Joseph Fanning and a mug shot of the bastard himself stare up at me. I consider Dana Reeves and Janie Hyatt. Is it possible these two average looking women—neither of whom looks particularly strong—could be holding Fanning for the purposes of torture or could have killed him already?

I've mapped out the route to the cabin Hyatt inherited. Maybe we'll get lucky and find Fanning there and wrap this one up tomorrow. I could take Friday off and get a few things done around here. God knows I have an avalanche of leave days built up even after all the time I took off with Stella.

My cell phone vibrates against the countertop. I answer with my usual, "Duncan."

The only sound on the other end is static. I frown. "Hello."

"Detective Walter Duncan?"

The voice is male. Not one I've heard before, that I can recall anyway. "That's me. What can I do for you?"

"This is Mario Sanchez."

The words break a little but I still hear and understand that this is the guy on a climbing trip down in Mexico. "Sanchez, thank you for calling."

I stay perfectly still just in case a movement in one direction or the other might cause the connection to drop off. I vividly remember back when most all long distance phone calls sounded like this.

"My wife says you've been very adamant about getting in touch with me."

The words crackle across the line in pieces but I get the gist of it.

"That's right. If you could call me as soon as you return home, I would appreciate it. I have a few questions I'd like to review with you in person. It's very important."

"That's the reason I'm calling. I wanted to confirm that we will return on Sunday and the minute I'm back in Nashville, I will call. Is there anything I can do from here, Detective? My wife was confused as to what this is about."

It was good to hear such eagerness to cooperate with the police though I'm not so sure he'll still feel that way when he learns all the fuss is about Fanning.

"Your wife tells me you and your friends left Nashville on Saturday morning and arrived in Mexico City late Sunday evening. Is that correct?"

"Yes, that's correct. We spent Saturday night in Brownsville, Texas, at a Holiday Inn Express."

"Your two friends were with you the whole time and can vouch for your itinerary?"

"Absolutely. This sounds serious, Detective. May I ask what this concerns?"

The static is back so I wait it out, hoping the call won't drop. "It's about Joseph Fanning, Mr. Sanchez."

The long stretch of dead air that follows makes me worry that he's severed the connection, then he says, "I see." He hesitates before going on. "Has he taken another victim?"

That is a tough one to answer. At this point we still can't say one way or the other. "We're not entirely sure, Mr. Sanchez. You see, he disappeared sometime between Sunday morning and midday on Monday. It's very important that we locate him."

More of that tense hush lingers between us; the crackle of static pops again and again. Finally, he speaks. "If the world is lucky, he's dead and buried somewhere."

I can't help wondering if that somewhere is in Mexico.

"Have a safe trip back, Mr. Sanchez. I look forward to hearing from you as soon as you're home."

The call ends and I study the photo of ten-year-old Mario Sanchez. He was Fanning's final victim. The one who fought back and won. But was the plea bargain Fanning managed to finagle for owning up to abusing all seventeen victims not what Sanchez had hoped for?

Or is the idea of his own child coming into the same world where Joseph Fanning lives too much for him to sit idly by and do nothing?

Would his friends help him take that kind of revenge?

I can't say just yet. I need to sit face to face with Sanchez and measure the man he has become. But I have already concluded one thing with absolutely certainty: There is no way a scrawny ten-year-old boy escaped Joseph Fanning without help. Both the detectives who worked the case felt Sanchez wasn't completely forthcoming but they had the bad guy so they let it go.

Maybe it's time that possibility was revisited.

I turn my attention to Reeves and Hyatt. There's always the chance Fanning is just a few miles up the road in Hendersonville hogtied in a shed or an old barn awaiting execution.

Somehow I can't muster up any sympathy.

He deserves a lot worse than whatever has happened to him.

THE CHILD

After the first year, I stopped thinking about my dead mother and my sorry, lowdown asshole of a father. They were no longer relevant and the thoughts only made me sad and miserable. I had a choice: I could hope to die or I could hope to survive.

I chose to survive.

The monster became my father, my mother, my world. I had no one else.

When I was nine years old, he started to allow me outside whatever shithole we lived in. Don't get me wrong, it didn't happen often but when it did it was like going to the circus for a kid who'd spent the past two years as a prisoner. He made sure my hair was brushed and even tucked a little pink barrette on one side. As we left the car and walked into the market or wherever, he held my hand, smiling like a proud daddy. It wasn't like he had to worry that someone would recognize me from a milk carton. No one had reported me missing. No one cared. I belonged to him.

The first time out in public was the most difficult. Not because I misbehaved but because I was terrified that someone else would take me. I'd lived through it once; I didn't want to risk going through it again. I needed the stability. As foolish as it sounds now, at the time I knew where my next meal would come from and that I would be warm on a cold night. I was well acquainted with the things he would do to me whenever he chose and, though I hated every second of it, I understood that I would survive those awful things. I'd learned to go to my happy place while he took what he wanted, to tune out his sickening grunting and the disgusting things he did to my skinny little body.

It was my new normal. My everyday routine.

Food and warmth and routines…those things were all that mattered to a nine-year-old who'd been sold like a pair of old shoes at a tag sale and who had been sexually abused in every possible way one can imagine.

You might think it's impossible to do all the things to a small child one can do to an adult, but you're wrong. Trust me when I say he did things to me that I will never share with anyone. Things no one can ever know because I cannot bear the reliving long enough to tell the story.

Between nine and ten our relationship began to shift somewhat. He realized he could use me for more than entertainment. No one worried when a child wandered too close to a shopping cart, or bumped against the heavy purse hanging from a shoulder or arm. I learned the art of pickpocketing like other kids learn how to ride a bike. It still amazes me the stash of cash most women kept handy in those days. It was as if they feared the need for change or a few dollars while attempting to exit a public parking garage with two sleeping kids in car seats. Or worse, the five bucks they used their debit card for at McDonald's would end up part of a major card security breach that required new debit cards and pin numbers. Always a pain in the ass.

Since there was inevitably the risk I might be caught by a shopper who wasn't as distracted as I first believed, he taught me how to avoid being trapped into a confession. How to lie like a pro. How to make the same lady I'd just robbed believe perhaps she was wrong after all. When all else failed there was the ace up my sleeve—the sympathy card. I was hungry. My baby sister needed milk. And then, of course, I learned how to evade capture. I could slip away and hide where no one would find me better than Houdini himself.

But stealing wasn't my only skill. I was also very, very good at begging in a way that didn't actually give the appearance of begging. I would stare, big eyed, at something most kids my age took entirely for granted—like a new pair of sneakers or a cute pair of jeans or a dress. I never bothered with toys. I had been taught they were pointless. I still had the teddy bear but he didn't actually count. On those occasions when I set out to get something only I wanted, I wore my most ragged clothes. *He* didn't teach me this technique; this is one I developed on my own. Even the hardest heart could be melted by a poor, dirty child in need. Children are starving all over the country and no one wants to hear about it. Put one in front of their faces so they have to look at it and all bets are off. They can't take it.

Funny thing was, I had no idea at the time that I was learning the skills I would desperately need later.

He still got angry and forced me into the dreaded box from time to time. And he kept me illiterate. He refused to teach me to read or to write. Too afraid, I suppose, that I would turn out smarter than him and then maybe figure out that I didn't really belong to him. The problem is, by age ten I didn't remember who I was. I was the child. *His* child. I belonged to him, body and soul.

During the rare occasion when I had to flee a pickpocket situation, it never once entered my mind to find a police officer or to tell someone I needed help. I was far more afraid of what might happen if I did this than I was of anything else he might possibly do to me. I had survived the worst he could possibly do to me.

Or, at least, I thought I had.

"I saved you."

My attention jerks to the piece of shit huddled in the darkest corner of his prison. Ah, so he's decided to talk today, has he?

"You saved me?" I scoff at the concept. Obviously his brain was damaged during all those years in prison.

I walk closer to where he huddles. I am not afraid. In addition to having a wide, ugly wound on his upper arm, he's bruised and battered quite thoroughly. As I approach him he shudders visibly and draws into a tighter ball. How pathetic. I think of all the times he beat me far more brutally than what I have done to him. I think of the endless ways he used my frail, tender body as a seven-year-old child and the need to kill him now—this instant—surges until my heart is thundering in my chest.

"You beat and raped me day after day, week after week, year after year until I was fifteen years old. What the hell do you think you saved me from?"

It doesn't matter really, what he thinks. He is nothing. Less than nothing. I have no idea why I bother interacting with him. Perhaps on some level I am curious how such a monster can believe himself the victim after what he has done. Or more to the point, how could he possibly do the things he did to me or to any other child and believe he deserves anything less than every ounce of pain I am capable of inflicting?

How has he lived with the memories of his grievous acts against the weakest members of society?

And why did he come back to Nashville? He could have gone to Murfreesboro or farther north. I suspect I know the answer to that one but we'll see.

"I saved you from the people who brought you into this world. Your mother was a junkie whore who killed herself for the sake of pleasure." Even as he boasts he braces for my retaliation.

Coward.

I consider kicking him in the side. I've done this numerous times already. Why bother? My mother was a junkie whore who chose her own selfish needs over mine. My father wasn't any better. He sold me to this depraved animal rather than deal with his drug addiction. He lasted a few months longer than my mother before he hit rock bottom and overdosed, but an extra few months of survival doesn't make him better.

"Do you know what today is?" I ask him rather than kick him as I first considered.

He shakes his head, fear filling his pathetic eyes. I do not possess the proper words to articulate how very much that fear pleases me.

"It's day three of our reunion," I say. "I'm surprised you didn't think of this when you were planning this elaborate game you set in motion. Do you remember what you did to me on day three after you took me home with you?"

He shakes his head adamantly at first and then the movement subsides as the memories flood his wretched brain. The fear tightens around his throat and chest in a chokehold. I hear the change in his respiration. See the growing terror in his eyes.

Oh, how it pleases me.

"But don't worry. I'm sure you were raped plenty of times in prison." I shrug. "Statistics show that men like you were probably raped as children, too. Is that true? Did your daddy or an uncle, maybe a grandpa, rape you as a child? Is that what turned you into the disgusting perv you became?"

He looks away. In all the years we were together he never spoke of the men in his family. There had to be men. He spoke only of his mother—the one who died of heart failure when he was just eight years old. Before he dies I'm going to tell him about searching until I found where his mother was buried. I went to her grave in the middle of the night and shit on it. Probably wasn't her fault he turned out the way he did since she died when he was so young, but she was the one who spit him out of her loins. For that, she deserved to be shit on, alive or dead.

"I'll make this a lot easier on you if you just tell me the truth."

After he was taken away to prison, I watched the news. I heard the armchair shrinks create scenarios based on his known history. His father had gotten himself murdered when Fanning was seventeen. His grandfather had been in a nursing home with Alzheimer's. When Fanning was nineteen, somehow his grandfather ended up dead in the shower at the care facility where he was a resident. Strange thing. The staff had no idea how he got out of bed and into the shower, much less fell and bashed his head on the tile. The shrinks speculated that the grandfather had molested Fanning as a child.

The monster remains silent, hovering in that corner like a trapped animal.

"We both know it was your grandfather. That's why you killed him." I experience much pleasure at saying these things to him. I want him to feel the way I felt. The worthlessness, the humiliation, the desolation. The utter uncertainty.

"Then why ask?" he snarls.

I smile. "I just want to hear you say the words, that's all. I want to hear all the terrible things he did to you. Maybe see if you learned those nasty tricks of yours from him."

"Shut up!"

The hoarse shriek gives me another shot of immense pleasure.

I really don't need any answers from him, I know how the story likely went. Does his damaged childhood make me feel the least bit sorry for him?

No.

He chose to continue the vicious cycle of abuse. Since he didn't have children of his own, he abused other people's children.

That is never going to happen again.

Never, ever, ever.

THURSDAY, MAY 3

DETECTIVE OLIVIA NEWHOUSE

"Sounds like she accepted your apology," Walt notes with a quick glance at me before making the turn onto McMurtry Road.

I toss my cell onto the console. What else can I do? I did exactly as I promised David I would. I called his mother. She was, as always, charming and accommodating. "Who knows? You can't ever tell with her."

David's mother would never allow her composure to slip or any sort of improper emotion to show. Not to me. I hesitate, feel bad for half a second for holding this uncomfortable situation against her when I was the no-show at dinner last night. But then, it's true. I met David's parents not long after we started dating. I've known them for approximately six months and I still feel like an outsider. My future mother-in-law is one of those people whose social graces are so ingrained that she would smile at the devil himself if he showed up at a function as long as his name was on the guest list. She was probably holding the phone tight enough to crack it as she listened to my feeble excuse for not attending the family dinner. Tracking down a missing pedophile couldn't possibly be more important than one of her family dinners.

A good future daughter-in-law would be looking for a way to make it up to her. I'm certain she views the situation from that prospective.

I fear I will never be what she considers a good daughter-in-law.

Maybe I'm overreacting. Maybe it's easier to believe they don't like me and then I don't have to feel guilty when I let them down. David has said this to me frequently since I moved into his house. I wonder if this is the pattern for the rest of our lives together. I think of this baby growing inside me and I am suddenly extremely anxious. A child needs a happy home without all this tension and frustration.

"She doesn't like you?"

I push away the thoughts of the future and almost laugh. "I really can't say for sure. I think they're still shocked David and I didn't fizzle out after a few weeks. I'm reasonably certain they had a family meeting and concluded I was a momentary blip on his radar—a rebound adventure after he and his longtime, more appropriate girlfriend ended their relationship."

Walt grunts. He would just as soon see me single and happy again. I shake my head and focus on the landscape as we maneuver onto Hogan Branch

Road. It is true that I'm happiest when it's just the work and me. Got that from my dad. I'm not sure I'm capable of changing a part of me so deeply engrained. Probably embedded in my genes.

First thing this morning I made up my mind not to mention anything about yet another headache to Walt. He worries about me too much as it is. Besides, how could I explain that not long after David and I made love, the agony woke me up from a dead sleep? That has never happened before. I was sleeping like a baby. I retreated to the guest room and shut out all light and all sound to get through the night. Rather than explain it to David, I left before he came downstairs this morning. I couldn't possibly tell him that after our beautiful lovemaking I grew immensely ill.

What is happening to me?

And when did I become such a coward?

"Here we go." Walt navigates his SUV across a narrow stream that flows over a dip in the long gravel driveway.

The cabin belonging to Janie Hyatt sits about a quarter mile beyond the stream, even farther from the road and surrounded by thick woods. The driveway bends around a small pond with a short dock jutting out over the still surface. A fishing boat floats in the water, one end tied to the dock. From all appearances it's the typical log cabin with a screened in front porch overlooking a tranquil pond. The perfect getaway from the noise and stress of city life.

"Nice place," Walt says.

"Yeah." I reach for the door and climb out. No vehicles around. "I wonder if anyone's home?"

"Doesn't look that way," Walt says, mostly to himself.

I scan the tree line as we move toward the cabin. Leaves flutter with the sudden movement of a bird. I watch it soar across the clear sky and disappear from sight. The quiet reminds me of the farm. Somewhere miles away I hear the sound of a car.

"So I've been looking for a retirement place," Walt announces. He flashes me a grin and a wink.

"Good one." We both know he's planning a move to Florida but the cover is a solid one. If anyone shows up, we're obviously lost. Just out driving around looking for the cabin we saw on some real estate site. What man wouldn't love his own little fishing hole right off the front porch? Surely this perfect place is for sale.

We separate and move around opposite ends of the cabin. No shed or barn or other structure. Just the cabin. On the east end, the one I round, there's the massive stone chimney. The screened porch wraps around the west end—the end Walt is covering—and comes to a stop just past the back door. Since most of the windows are concealed by the presence of the screened porch, I climb the back steps.

"I'll see if anyone's home," I say as if I fully expect the owner to answer the door and usher us inside for sweet tea.

Walt nods and heads back around front. He'll go to the front door. It's our usual routine. One goes to the back door, the other goes to the front. On the porch the flowers in the pewter pitcher standing on the table between two chairs are still alive. I check the water level in the pitcher, hall full. Someone has been here recently.

I open the screen door and rap on the wood door behind it. I lean closer and peer through the glass. A small kitchen that leads into the living room. I can see the big fireplace and a couple of comfy looking chairs flanking it. It's quiet inside. On a side table in the living room the screen on the small television is black. I hear Walt knocking on the front door. I should move on to the next window but instead I pull my sleeve down over my hand and turn the doorknob.

The door opens.

"Hmm." Now that's a surprise.

Going inside without exigent circumstances or a warrant is against the law. I remind myself of this fact even as I cross the threshold. Walt would say the same thing if he were standing next to me, but he's not. If there's anyone in the house, I'll just say the door was standing ajar and I was concerned.

I drag a pair of latex gloves from my jacket pocket and pull them on as I walk across the uncluttered kitchen. The cabin is small. Can't be more than four rooms. It'll take barely a minute to walk through the floor plan. Fridge is empty except for an opened block of cheese and a half empty bottle of wine. Stove is cold. No dishes in the sink. I move to the living room. No ash in the fireplace. The temps have been fairly low at night. Anyone staying here would have needed a fire. I pass into a short hall. Three doors, the narrowest one is obviously a closet. I open it first. Shelves loaded with linens and other household goods. The second door is a small bathroom. A good size bedroom is behind the final door. Bed is made. No one hiding underneath it. No one in that dinky closet either.

Walt is in the kitchen when I make my way back there. "Nothing?" he asks.

I shake my head. "You find anything?"

"I opened the door to the crawlspace. No hidden basement." He peels off his gloves. "Just the usual. Spiders and crickets."

"We should take a look around beyond the tree line." I survey the main living area one last time. "Make sure there's not an underground storm shelter or a root cellar. Or one of those bug out hidey holes."

He nods. "That's about all we can do."

It takes a solid two hours to have a good look around. If there's an underground bunker of some sort, we couldn't find any indication of a fresh air access or an entrance. No newly turned earth. None of the vegetation appears to have been disturbed. If Hyatt and Reeves killed Fanning, they buried him so deep in the woods we'll never find his body without ground radar.

At the front of the house I consider the pond. It's possible they dumped him in the water. I walk out onto the small dock; the boards creak and sigh as if no one has disturbed them in a while. I scan the shimmering surface. Doesn't look that deep but I don't think I want to dive in and find out. The water would be as cold as ice.

"Thinking of taking a swim?" Walt joins me at the dock.

"I'll pass." I turn to him. "We're closing in on the end of our list with nothing to show for it. Maybe we're focused on the wrong victims."

If Fanning took a victim, getting injured in the process, he would be too scared to go back home. That's a given. He would hide until he was found or escaped to someplace far away. The only question is: where would he hide? He has no living family. Certainly no friends. I can't see him lying low with a friend anyway. Fanning is a loner. Based on his file, he always worked alone and he never ran. According to his own statements, he'd lived in and around Nashville his whole life. The experts agreed that every child he took without getting caught made him braver and braver.

Cocky son of a bitch.

My stomach growls. I turn to my partner. "We should grab some lunch and follow up on those two new names that popped up on the missing persons list."

"Sounds good to me," Walt agrees.

Personally, I need a break from focusing totally on Fanning. The two kids who only this morning were reported as missing are older, a sixteen and a seventeen-year-old. Fanning didn't generally hunt in that age group, but he's been in prison a long time. His tastes or his ability to wait out the perfect prey may have changed.

As Walt drives back toward Nashville, I find myself obsessing about David and his family again. I love him. I do. Sometimes I feel completely certain that I want to marry him. Then those doubts creep back in. Will I get used to his family and their overly pretentious ways? I can't comprehend why I suddenly feel incapable of relating to them. Of fitting in. I've never experienced such a lack of confidence. And if I can't see my way past all that, what about the baby? What do I do from here?

For starters, I don't sell the farm. I may end up needing to go back there to live. It's a good place for kids. Quiet, peaceful. There are no horses anymore but that can change. I cannot imagine in a million years homeschooling my child as my parents did me, which is okay because the farm is located in a good school district.

Could I be a good mother? My mother was a great mother. She died when I was twenty-three, but my father and I made it a point to speak of her often. Recalled all the fun times. He would not allow her memory to die. He made sure I never forgot no matter how busy I was with work. He reminded me of the family life we shared. Maybe keeping all those memories in front of me was his way of ensuring he never forgot a single moment either. He was a dedicated, loving husband, father and doctor.

Though he didn't have an opportunity to get to know David until just a couple of months before his death, he liked him. I had the impression he approved of our fledgling relationship. I wish there had been more time.

I glance at Walt. I wonder if a man like David can possibly ever be the sort of caring man my father was, that Walt is. I'm not so sure men like them exist anymore. A dying breed.

Walt's gray hair is mussed on one side from our trek through the woods. I smile and resist the urge to reach over and smooth it. I don't want to embarrass him. He'll glance in the mirror and notice eventually.

My thoughts shift back to David. No, he is not like my father or Walt. Chances are, he won't ever be. But then I'm not exactly the storybook picture of a wife. I suppose I'm about as far from June Cleaver as is possible to get and still be a member of the female species. Which begs the question of my nurturing skills.

Too late to worry about that now.

When I snap out of my daze I realize we're already at the first of the two addresses we need to visit. At the top of our list is Chloe Simone, sixteen years old.

The Simone home is a small white bungalow with green shutters and a wide porch. The houses along the block are shoehorned next to each other with barely a strip of grass between them. It's an older neighborhood with mature trees and no shortage of deferred maintenance. Chloe lives with her grandmother since her parents died in a house fire when she was only ten. She's an honor student at her school and has lots of friends. The girl's grandmother gave her free rein to roam the neighborhood as long as her homework was done and her grades were in order. Brighter than average, Chloe had all the free time in the world to wander to her heart's desire. And now she's missing.

Posters, flowers and stuffed animals surround a shrine started in Chloe's front yard. *Please send Chloe home! Help us find Chloe! God will bring Chloe home.*

Unfortunately unless her abductor suddenly grows a conscience and drops her off somewhere or by sheer luck she escapes, the only way she is coming home is if the cops working on her case find her in time or via the morgue. At this point, to believe anything else is wishful thinking. Even the small reward offered for information on the missing girl will likely be futile. Chloe Simone has been missing for twice that critical forty-eight hours. The grandmother mistakenly thought the class trip was this week. It wasn't until one of Chloe's friends showed up looking for her that the grandmother realized her mistake. According to the police report, the poor grandmother is beside herself. She has not laid eyes on the child since Sunday morning and hope is dwindling.

Sadly she has good reason to be afraid. Chloe's odds of being found alive have diminished considerably over the past twenty-four hours. Even Fanning never kept a victim more than a few hours. Thankfully, none of his—as far as we know—were murdered.

Unless his MO has changed this time or some aspect of his strategy has gone terribly, terribly wrong, hopefully he hasn't killed anyone. I think of the blood at his duplex. He's been out of the game for a long while. His abduction skills are no doubt rusty. A fatal accident may have occurred.

Then again, there's always the possibility that he has suddenly decided to keep a victim, hiding in plain sight as he did before. Still, keeping a sixteen or seventeen-year-old victim compliant wouldn't be an easy task.

Milton Simone, the grandfather, answers the door. Walt does the introductions and we're promptly invited in. My partner begins with the expected questions. How are they holding up? Is there anything else the police should be doing that they are not? Can we get them anything they might need? Walt knows the manager at the local Kroger. He can have anything they need delivered.

The elderly couple assures us they're fine and that they have everything they need, except their granddaughter. A framed photo of Chloe sits on the coffee table surrounded by lit prayer candles and the family's Bible. The Book is dog-eared and visibly worn from use.

"Mr. and Mrs. Simone," I ask, "have any of Chloe's friends mentioned seeing her with an older man?"

Chloe's friends and classmates, as well as the neighbors, have all been questioned endlessly about any strangers who might have been lurking in the neighborhood or around the school. So far nothing has emerged in all the questioning. Chloe has no enemies. No trouble at school, none at home. She is happy. Her parents' deaths were years ago and from all appearances she has adjusted well to living with her grandparents. Her pay as you go cell phone hasn't been found and the laptop issued by the school is now at Metro's crime lab for processing. The crime scene investigators combed through her social media pages but found nothing of interest. A friend last saw her on Sunday evening just before dark in the parking lot of the apartment building at the end of the block. Several of her classmates live in those apartments.

Mrs. Simone shakes her head adamantly. "Chloe would never let herself be fooled by offers of gifts or money. We taught her to beware of strangers. If she got into a car with a stranger then she did so unconscious or kicking and screaming. There is zero chance it happened any other way."

Her voice wavers on the last.

I nod, summon an encouraging smile that I in no way feel. "You taught her well."

The Simones have already been shown a photo of Fanning. They both stated they had never seen him before.

"The police still think it might be related to that man—this Fanning?" Mr. Simone asks.

"We're following up on every possible avenue," Walt explains. "The fact that Fanning disappeared at approximately the same time gives us reason to believe there might be a connection but that is the only related thread we have. No other evidence or statements suggest he was seen with your granddaughter."

"There was that one girl," Mr. Simone says to his wife. "You know the one who told you she thought an old man had been hanging around the apartments. She said he was watching her and Chloe."

Mrs. Simone shook her head. "You're thinking about the janitor they used to have at the school. He's retired now. They got a new one," she reminded him. "The police already checked him out. Detective Renault said they ruled him out."

I remember reading the statement from a janitor. He had an airtight alibi. Just an old man who likes ogling females of any age.

Walt places his business card on the table. "Please call us if you think of anything else or if one of Chloe's friends comes to you with any new information."

The Simones promise to do so and we leave. I glance around the rundown neighborhood. The Simones are clinging to the last vestiges of their optimism about their granddaughter but I have a bad feeling this will not end well.

"You said Sanchez will be back on Sunday," I comment as we climb into the Tahoe. "You going to call me when he calls you?"

Walt starts the engine and shifts into Drive. "You know it, partner."

Frankly, it seems like a bit of a moot effort since Sanchez has been out of town since before Fanning went missing. But Walt doesn't want to mark him off the list until he's interviewed him face to face.

That's because Walt is a good cop.

A damned good cop.

I'm still trying to figure out why the guy's name sounds familiar to me. Too many other things going on to obsess about it. I guess I'll find out on Sunday.

At the end of the day I am spent. Walt and I interviewed the parents of the other missing teenager, Suzy Eldridge, and then one more name on our list of Fanning's past victims. The latter was yet another harrowing account of the worst one human can do to another. I am amazed all over again at how a man like Fanning got off with only thirteen years and change in prison. Plea bargains save the courts money, ensure a conviction. I understand this. Still, it's a travesty. One, I suspect, is being amended. I push away the images of his torture that instantly come to mind.

As a cop, I'm disappointed at the prospect that someone has taken the law—justice—into his or her own hands. Conversely, as a human I'm thrilled that anyone had the balls not to let this go. My father would say it's the universal issue of civilized society. As humans our basic instinct is survival and self-protection. The rules of society push us to forgive, to turn the other cheek...to give a slap on the wrist to the evil among us and carry on. All will be well.

But evil doesn't live by society's rules. Evil lives for one simple purpose: to fulfill its selfish desires, whatever the cost to others.

Joseph Fanning is pure evil. No matter, society's rules dictate that Walt and I must find him and protect him if need be or arrest him if he's committed some crime. We are no closer to accomplishing one or the other than we were seventy-odd hours ago when this case landed in our laps.

No matter that I've been late every night for days. No matter that David will be home soon, instead of going to his house I go to the farm where I was raised. Half an hour commute from Nashville into the horse country of Franklin.

Am I avoiding the man I love? The man I'm supposed to marry? Yes. If I avoid him I don't have to reveal my fears and uncertainty about us, about the baby. I can pretend I'm too busy to go into such a profoundly life changing discussion at the moment. Life will be calmer when this case is solved and David and I can discuss and plan for this new reality at that point.

He wants children. We haven't discussed the when, but that's irrelevant now.

I unlock the house, step inside and disarm the security system, then close my eyes and inhale deeply the scent of home. I'm not sure how many years it will take for me to see anyplace else as home. I know it happens. People marry and leave home and start their own homes. But some part of where you came from is always home, I think.

David is intent on me selling this place. The house is so big and there's more than forty acres of woods and pastures. Someone who has horses should have the place, he reminds me. Someone who has the time to appreciate the property and all its natural majesty. He's right, I suppose, but I can't imagine not having this place to escape to whenever I feel the need.

Like now.

Walt suggested I lease the land and keep the house for a getaway from the city. Lots of Nashvillians have country houses or lake houses. No reason I can't keep it. It's mine. It's paid for. I open my eyes and survey the massive great room that serves as the centerpiece of this house. Any way I look at it, this is home. Large and airy but not the slightest bit ostentatious.

I lock the door behind me and wander through the room. Those damn packing boxes are scattered everywhere. I feel ashamed that I even started the process of packing up my parents' things. It's too soon. I shouldn't have listened to David. Since I didn't argue with him on the subject I can't blame him. If I don't want to sell the house or pack up their things all I have to do is say so.

The past is the past, Liv. Living there can sometimes be a futile and harmful thing.

My father reminded me often that though it was perfectly fine to feel wistful about the past, particularly lost loved ones, it was never smart to linger there unless it was in the good memories. *The past is the past for a reason,* he would say. *It's behind you. Move toward what's in front of you, Liv.*

But it's the past that has drawn me back here today. Right after my father's death, it was necessary to pull out his will and other essential papers and to go through his office. He'd had a number of those necessary documents laid out on his desk already. I don't know whether he was feeling ill and just didn't tell me or if he was merely doing an annual update to his paperwork. Some financial records and insurance documents were out of their folders. A sealed envelope that contained a letter of instruction, reminding me where important documents were stored, the names of insurance companies, passwords for bank accounts and other online accounts had been right on top. He made sure the instructions were as easy to follow as a detailed road map.

I walk beyond the cavernous great room and into the side hall that leads to his home office and on to the master suite. My father loved his office. It looks out over the rolling green pastures of the property. Those pastures spill out around the front and west side of the house's perch on a rise. Behind the house are acres and acres of woods. I loved exploring those woods when I was younger.

I round his desk, pull out his Herman Miller chair and sit. My father swore these were the most comfortable chairs on the market. After spending so much time at his desk going through the estate papers, I have to agree.

The files are neatly arranged. Most are personal files related to his finances and the property and all that it entails. All but a few I pulled from where they were stored as I prepared for settling the estate. I've been through those repeatedly. Across the room the row of steel cabinets house his professional case files. There are certain steps that need to be taken on those files. He left specific instructions. Just something else I need to get around to. I open the center drawer of his desk and retrieve the notes I stuffed there after removing them from the trash bin under his desk. The day he had the heart attack he'd been right here at this desk, cleaning out some of his drawers apparently.

I didn't find out until after the funeral that he had been having some heart issues. I found the prescriptions and visited his doctor, a family friend. He hadn't said anything at the funeral because he assumed I knew. But my father never told me. Didn't want to worry me, I suppose. He was always far too concerned with ensuring I was happy to tell me bad news. I could never understand why he viewed me as so fragile. I'm strong. I'm a cop—a homicide detective.

Even if these migraines have kicked my butt recently.

So far, so good today. Any aches I've suffered have been a distant twinge. I mentally cross my fingers.

My intention is to go through everything—eventually—and burn all the papers that were related to his work or finances that he appeared not to want or need—which is what he wanted according to the letter of instruction. Discounting, of course, the official patient files. Those are the ones with the precise instructions on disposition. Anything else I deem simple rubbish I will toss in the bin and burn. I probably would have burned the pages of notes I found in the bin under his desk if I hadn't noticed a name. At the time the name wasn't one I recognized but I worried that it was either a patient or a work-related associate. It wasn't until Walt mentioned that Sanchez would be home from Mexico on Sunday that the memory finally clicked.

So maybe I didn't come here after work to avoid David. Maybe I came in search of some truth that will help us solve this case. Only *this* doesn't feel like a simple, unexpectedly discovered truth. This feels like a stumbled upon, well-hidden secret.

I open the papers and confirm that nagging worry: the name on my father's tossed handwritten notes is *Mario Sanchez*. Under normal circumstances this wouldn't exactly be a stunning revelation. He treated hundreds of patients in the Nashville area over the course of his long and prestigious career. But this is not just any name, this is a name on Walt's and my list of persons of interest.

I skim through the notes once more in search of any other names I might have overlooked. I reach the last page and my gaze stalls. Letters—initials possibly. Two simple pieces of the alphabet that were jotted next to each other shock the breath out of me.

JF.

Joseph Fanning.

I call Walt.

DETECTIVE WALTER DUNCAN

I park next to Liv's Subaru. She waits at the front door of the house, leaning against the jamb, arms crossed over her chest.

She knows before I get out of the car the things I'll ask first and she's ready to defend her feelings and choices. *You feeling okay?* I'm fine, she would say. You don't need to worry about me. A little headache isn't going to keep me down. *Have you been home?* Aghast, she would demand, how is that relevant? I'll get there when I get there. I called you here for an important reason, Walt.

I know her almost as well as I know myself. I'll bet she hasn't been home yet. It's almost seven. The fact that she's still wearing the gray jacket and black trousers she wore to work today tells me I would win that bet. I wonder if she's even called him. As much as I dislike the knucklehead, I know she loves him. I just can't figure out why she's working so hard to push him away. Even when I play devil's advocate, she won't exactly say she doesn't love him or that she wants to end the relationship. She's confused and feeling uncertain.

Then again, he does make it a relatively simple reflex to push him away. He just can't help himself when it comes to trying to control every last detail of her life. If Stella were here she'd tell me to mind my own business.

"But she's like a daughter to me," I mumble.

Stella would say I know.

I climb out of the Tahoe and amble across the yard. "Traffic was murder." This is my excuse for taking an entire forty-five minutes to get here when I was actually following up with Reynolds to see if he had anything back on the DNA from the scene. Sometimes a face-to-face works far better than a phone call. It wasn't my intent to put Liv off. Absolutely not. I guess I just feel guilty for making that planned stop even after she called.

Then again, she hadn't said to hurry. She hadn't even sounded worried, just distant and distracted somehow.

Ultimately the visit to Reynolds was a waste of time. He did not have the DNA reports back yet. Furthermore, he had nothing relevant from the numerous pieces of trace evidence the crime scene folks had spent hours collecting at the scene. White cotton, potentially from a sheet or other piece of linen. A hair that belonged to Fanning. Some animal fecal matter that likely got tracked in on Fanning's or the perp's/vic's shoes. One of the neighbor's dogs liked taking dumps in any yard but his own.

Reynolds had nothing that would help us determine what the hell happened to the bastard.

The worst part is that we still can't be certain Fanning is even the victim. He could be the perpetrator of whatever took place in that dump he calls home. Either way, someone—two someones, actually—were injured and we need to figure out what happened. Hopefully while we can still make a difference.

"You okay?" I ask this expected question as I climb the steps up to the porch.

As I take the final step a weariness washes over me and I resist the urge to sit down right there and just lean against the railing. I am tired. More tired than I have felt since those all night vigils with Stella. I'd work all day while the nurse sat with her and then I'd spend the night entertaining her or just watching her breathe. I was terrified that if I closed my eyes I'd wake up and she'd be gone.

"I don't know," Liv admits. "Okay is suddenly complicated."

These words surprise me. Liv isn't one to bemoan her lot in life. If she's having a bad day she usually pretends it's merely challenging or that she has no idea what I'm talking about. She keeps her chin up. Always. Even, I've learned lately, when one of those headaches kicks her butt. Frankly, the worries she recently voiced about Preston are unusual. I can't help wondering if something more is going on.

"How complicated?" I pause at the door as she steps aside to let me in.

"You should have a drink."

"Oh." I groan. "That complicated."

Liv is not a drinker. The occasional glass of wine or beer but she's way too level headed to go overboard with either. Never smoked. Runs and works out. Eats all those natural colorful veggies they say are good for you. The list of healthy stuff she does makes me exhausted just thinking about it.

I lower myself onto Dr. Newhouse's leather sofa. Liv rounds the bar and pours me a Scotch. My mouth waters. This won't be the cheap stuff. Her daddy bought only the best. She returns to where I wait but she's carrying only one drink.

"What about you?" I accept the glass she offers.

"That's part of the complication."

I knock back a slug of the scotch, clear my throat. "All right. I'm listening."

Liv sits down on the coffee table, her chin in her hands, elbows on her knees. "All these migraines and feeling utterly exhausted all the time really had me worried. And I was late." She glances up at me and I nod in understanding. "So I took a pregnancy test and it was positive. That's really why I went to the doctor. With all the headaches I thought something might be wrong."

The wind goes right out of my sails. I'm nodding again, like a cheap bobblehead doll. "What does your fiancé have to say about this?"

I recognize my tone is accusing as if the man has done something bad and needs taking down a couple of notches. When she smiles some of the heaviness lifts from my chest.

"You're the only person besides my doctor who knows."

My smile turns into a grin. "He won't like that you told me first."

She rolls her eyes. "That's the least of my worries. I don't know if I'm properly equipped to be a mother, Walt. This is seriously complicated."

I reach out, take her hand in mine. "First, yes it's complicated but it's also amazing and crazy wonderful. Stella and I wanted children so badly. It's a blessing. After losing your father, it's a miracle. That's what it is. Second, you'll be an incredible mother. The best. No question."

"I wish I could feel as sure as you do."

My mind goes back to the logistics of all this. "So is the pregnancy causing the headaches?"

I'm hoping the answer is yes and that there isn't some other underlying issue.

"Dr. Raeford said it's a combination of the pregnancy hormones, and all the loss and stress I've experienced lately. She thinks it'll pass or at least ease up in the next few weeks as I move into the second trimester."

Regret and sadness gore me. "So when is this baby due? I have to start making plans, kid."

"December fourteenth, give or take a few days. We'll know more after an ultrasound." She shakes her head. "Merry Christmas to me."

The pages of the calendar—the days, weeks, months—whirl in my head. The chances of me making it that long are slim to none. For the first time since I came to terms with my terminal prognosis, I want to howl in misery. The idea of not being here to see Liv's baby rips my heart into shreds. The urge to tell her I'm dying is nearly overwhelming but I will not put that pain on top of all that she's suffered this year already. No way. Not until I have no choice.

She deserves happiness. I refuse to be the reason even a smidgeon of that happiness is tarnished right now. My own complicated news will come soon enough.

I square my shoulders and do the fatherly thing. "You have to talk to Preston about this. It's not right to leave him out."

"I know." She nods. "I will talk to him, I promise. I just need to get used to the idea myself before I go there. He'll want to tell his parents and, well, you understand. Particularly right now, with this case. I just can't handle all that."

I do understand. "So, how does he feel about dogs?"

I can't exactly ask her to take Sandy without telling her the reason. For now, feeling out how her future husband might react to having a pet around the house will have to do. If I die before we have the second part of the conversation, she'll look back on this moment and realize why I was asking.

To explain my reason for asking, I add, "You know they say men who like animals make better fathers." I have no idea if this is true but it seems reasonable.

"He loves dogs." She says this as if she finds the answer surprising herself. "He had a border collie for twelve years, she died just before he and I met. He hasn't had the heart to get another one." A smile tugs at her lips. "So I guess that's a good sign."

I nod, relieved. "Definitely a good sign."

"There's more." She stands. "This is complicated in a different way. I need you to look at something for me."

"Okay." This does sound ominous. I stand, leaving my glass on the coffee table, and follow her across the room and down the hall. In her father's office, she crosses to the desk and picks up a few pages of paper that look as if they've been crumpled and then smoothed out.

"You starting with your father's office on your packing or was he doing some housekeeping before he passed?" Doesn't take a crystal ball to see either scenario is possible. There are a couple packing boxes taped and ready to fill on the floor. Several file folders lay in a neat stack on the desk.

"A little of both." She hands me the pages. "There are several notes about a man he spoke with or treated." She shrugs. "Or had some sort of relationship with."

I scan the first page, but don't see a name until I reach the second. My gaze crashes into hers. "Mario Sanchez."

"Yeah. The notes don't make a lot of sense. It's mostly dates and locations. But there are initials noted on that last page. I think he was referring to Fanning."

I scan the third page again, more slowly this time. I see what she means. *JF.* "Okay, I see it. The rest of the notations are mostly dates." The realization of what I'm looking at suddenly sinks in and I tap the page. "These are dates from the time period of Fanning's trial." The bastard was arrested in June, but he didn't go to trial until early the next year.

"Maybe my father evaluated the victims, assessed their reliability. Something like that."

"Have you found any files related to Fanning or Sanchez or any of the others?" I don't have to tell her that Dr. Newhouse's name is not in the official case file. If he was officially involved in any capacity, it was for the defense and was never revealed. Not something Liv will want to discover, I'm sure.

"Not so far." She turns to the row of filing cabinets on the far wall. "I've been through all those and there are no names from our list—unless the patients were listed under aliases. I suppose that's possible in which case I wouldn't know where to begin."

Before I can pull together a reasonable theory, she warns, "It gets worse. While I was waiting for you to get here I did a little more looking around." She picks up the leather bound calendar from her father's desk. As she shuffles through to find whatever she's looking for I see numerous notes on page after page. Like me, her father preferred making notes the old fashioned way.

"Have a look at this." She passes me the calendar.

I stare at January twentieth. Just over two weeks before her father died. *J. F. Riverbend.*

"Why in the world would my father visit Joseph Fanning in prison?"

Although, knowing her father, I'm certain there is a perfectly logical explanation, I can't for the life of me think what it would be.

"The JF on his calendar on that page might not be Joseph Fanning," I offer.

She cocks her head and gives me a look. "Get real, Walt. I guess the Mario Sanchez in those notations isn't the same one climbing mountains down in Mexico either."

"I guess we need to find out."

Maybe Liv and I aren't the only ones keeping secrets.

THE CHILD

I watch him sleep the sleep of sheer exhaustion—the sort that comes after endless hours of pain. The adrenaline of fear will keep one wide awake for long hours. It would be so easy for a victim to simply pass out and that does sometimes happen. But a true artist of pain knows just how far to go before that particular defense mechanism kicks in. If you fail, there's always the dash of cold water to get things going again. These things I learned from the master. Now the tables are turned. I wonder what he will learn from me?

I smile. I have only begun to hurt him. Before he takes his final breath, he will know all the pain and fear I knew.

The pain, the fear, the uncertainty. It was ruthless in the beginning. But I adapted. Like all things, with the passage of time the child I was when he first took me began to change. Time waits for no one, as they say. The buds of breasts started to burgeon from my flat chest. Hair thickened and darkened down below.

I hated it. Hated the breasts poking out. I didn't want those things. I wanted to stay a child. The world looks at a child as an innocent—no matter the things that happen behind closed doors. A child is revered in many ways. A child is forgiven for her trespasses.

A child is the universal symbol of hope for mankind.

However hard I tried to stop it, my childhood was abandoning me, leaving me like the skin of a snake being sloughed off because it couldn't stretch any further. I was becoming an *it*. Not a child, not a woman. An it, *his* it.

Ultimately I became whatever he wanted me to be, whenever he wanted. That was my sole mission in life. He warned that no matter how much I changed I would always be his. Until the end of time I would belong to him. Strangely, this warning was the most comforting words he ever said to me.

The breasts presented a problem for his plans as well. A child could far more easily pick the pockets of unsuspecting shoppers and pedestrians. People were far more likely to toss money to a child. He bought ace bandages for binding my chest. For a while that method worked. But eventually no amount of binding would conceal the hideous mounds growing on my torso. I hated them. Hated him for allowing it to happen. He was, after all, all powerful, the ruler of my universe. He should have been able to stop this disaster before it changed everything.

Except he couldn't. And one day another change occurred. I woke up with blood between my thighs. I screamed and cried, certain I was dying. He laughed at me, allowed me to huddle in fear for hours before he explained that this, too, was a natural progression of aging. He didn't actually explain why it was happening just that it was and that I could expect it to come again each month.

He insisted I use tampons and that I flush them down the toilet since he couldn't tolerate the putrid smell of the pads. I did as he instructed. For weeks after the first period I was terrified of what the changes to my body meant. I prayed for a miracle, though I didn't really understand what prayer was or to whom those prayers should be addressed. My parents never took me to church but I'd heard snatches of conversations where people might say, "I'll be praying for you." I'd even had people say to me, "Bless you child. I'll pray for you and your daddy."

I figured praying was something people did to make something happen, so I prayed the breasts would disappear and the blood would never come back.

But neither of those prayers was answered and I lived in new, abject fear of what might occur because of these changes. He still took my body whenever he wanted. That had not changed. But he did use a condom. He told me it was because of the blood. He didn't want my nastiness to get on him. This, too, worried me. Suddenly his grunting and disgusting actions became reassuring. This was my normal. Routine. Everything was okay no matter that I was changing. I needed him to still want me, to do with me as he pleased. It was the only gauge by which I could measure my worth to him. I was terrified at the idea that he might decide he no longer wanted or needed me. What would I do then?

How would I survive?

My newest second hand clothes quickly became too small. My hips grew wider and my thighs fuller, not to mention those damned breasts. Boys started to look at me. I was used to dirty old men looking at me, but now it was boys—boys my age. This made the monster angry. He hated when boys looked at me. He made me wear big coats even when it was too warm so they couldn't see my breasts. He didn't buy me shoes with heels anymore. He said I was getting too tall. Almost as tall as him even in flats.

The more I changed, the angrier he became.

My fear expanded and undulated inside me, eating away at any semblance of confidence I had developed. I was frantic to please him, to ensure my relevance in his shitty little world. Not only did I do whatever he asked, I begged him to tell me more ways I could be useful. That was when he started to use me to lure in the other children he wanted to play with. I hated that part the most of all. I hated that he turned to another child for what he had always taken from me. I hated that they were prettier, fresher and sweeter than me. He told me this over and over so it must have been true.

I hated him, hated the other children…hated me.

As the months and years dragged on, his frustration and anger with the changes happening to my body began to amuse me to some degree. I was his, he'd said so a million times. I would always be his. So, as far as I could see, he was stuck with this taller, curvier me.

Inside my head where he couldn't see or hear I would laugh when he struggled to make me look more childlike. I just stood there letting him bind my breasts and dress me as if I were a life-size doll.

I even heard other men ask him about me. How much did I cost for an hour? This seemed to outrage him. He would growl and make threats at these men for saying such things about his daughter. Then he would take me home and rut into me until he wasn't angry anymore.

My belief that his taking of my body and keeping me fed and warm meant that he loved me solidified each time he acted out his claim of possession. We were a family. Slowly but surely I learned again to trust this illusion without question. I had watched mothers and fathers with their children and even though he was never as kind and gentle as those people, he took care of me and for a girl who knew nothing better, that was important. No one else would do so—no one else ever had. As if his confidence was the one slipping now he reminded me over and over that no one would ever want me. I was ugly with pointy breasts and pimples popping out all over my skin.

Who would want such an ugly it?

He was right. I was grateful he wanted me.

Ultimately I learned something from the changes and his reactions to those changes. I didn't need to be scared anymore. He wasn't going to give me to anyone else. He wasn't going to sell me or leave me no matter how many other children he played with. In fact, since he had already done all those bad and hurtful things to me, there was really no reason at all for me to fear what he might do next.

Over the years I had survived the worst he could possibly do to me...or at least, I thought I had.

FRIDAY, MAY 4

DETECTIVE OLIVIA NEWHOUSE

I'm waiting for David when he comes down for his first cup of coffee. I'm dressed and ready for work, and on my third cup of caffeine-infused brew. Still forgot to Google whether or not it's possible to consume too much caffeine during pregnancy. I did remember to pick up the prenatal vitamins. Took my first one this morning. I really have to do better than this. Just because I'm screwing up my own health by not eating as I should and not getting nearly enough sleep doesn't mean I want to screw up this kid's chances at normal.

The word gives me pause. What is normal?

Images and voices filter through my mind, make my stomach churn.

"Morning," he says as he shuffles to the coffee maker.

"Morning."

I really had intended to talk to him when I made it home last night but he'd already gone to bed. It wasn't even midnight. That was really early for him. Unless he had some sort of big bankers meeting and was mentally wiped out. Judging by his bloodshot eyes I'm thinking he went a couple of rounds with something stronger than beer and it took him out. David isn't generally a heavy drinker. I suppose I've sent him down that dark path. Apparently I can't do anything right anymore.

Last night got away from me. I hadn't meant to be so late but after Walt left I just passed out for a few hours. I woke up face down on my father's desk, drooling all over his blotter pad. I need to ask the doctor about that, too. I went down for the count and slept the sleep of the dead for at least two hours. I guess I needed the rest.

Exhaustion can do strange things to you.

"We need to talk," I announce. My throat goes instantly dry and my heart starts to pound. Walt is right in that I need to tell David about the baby and somehow slow down this lunge toward disaster that our relationship appears to be caught up in. We're here and I've had some decent sleep. This is as good a time as any.

He waits until the final drops of coffee have plopped into his mug, picks it up and swallows a mouthful then flinches from the burn. "I have my own ideas about that, but what is it you think we have to talk about, Liv?"

"All we do lately is argue," I say, weary of this battle. He clearly went to bed angry with me and now he's awakened still angry. How are we supposed to get past this unhappy place if he's unwilling to move beyond it? I really have no idea how to begin.

He props a pajama-clad hip against the counter. "I suppose that's my fault, too."

Perfect example of why we can't get past this rut. "I apologized to your mother."

He sips his coffee, nods. "She told me."

"So you're still angry with me about missing dinner, even though I've apologized repeatedly."

"Where were you last night?" He looks directly at me as he asks this question. The accusation is stark in his beautiful eyes.

"Working. You know this without asking." I hold my own mug of coffee so tightly I fear it may crack at any second. "When I came home you were already in bed."

"You were at the farm."

For a moment I'm rattled that he somehow knows this when we haven't talked about exactly where I was. Has he been following me? Does he have someone else following me? "First, what difference does that make and, second, how can you know this? Do you have someone following me?"

"First," he echoes, his tone as sharp as a knife, "you just said you were working which was apparently a lie. Second, your iPad dinged with a notification that the security system at the farm had been disarmed. Is there anyone else who would be there?"

Okay. He has me there. I hesitate for a moment. Do I want to tell him about what I found? If I don't he's never going to trust me but to tell him feels like a betrayal of my father.

Stop, Liv. This is the man to whom you've said yes to spending the rest of your life. This is the father of the child you're carrying. Why the hesitation?

"I found some notes my father made regarding a victim in the Fanning case. I'm sure there's a perfectly logical reason for him being involved in any way but I have to know what that reason was."

"So your father is a person of interest in your investigation now?"

I think about that for a moment. "In a manner of speaking. We haven't found anything that concretely ties him to the case, but we have to look into whatever part he played."

"*We* meaning you and Walt?"

The sarcasm in his tone leaves me both baffled and angry. "He is my partner. How many times do I have to point out that fact?"

"So you and Walt were at the farm, *together.*"

Somehow he makes the detail sound lascivious. "When I found the notes I called him immediately. Making a judgment one way or the other about something my father did or didn't do in this situation would be the wrong thing to do. I'm personally involved, my objectivity is compromised."

"Aren't you and Walt personally involved?"

"What?" Obviously David really is only interested in fighting. "We're partners."

"And friends. Good friends. Isn't that personal?"

I slam my mug down on the counter. Coffee splatters. "I don't even know why I try. You want to fight. You don't want to understand what's happening with me right now."

He walks slowly toward me. Any other time I would have considered this sexy, but right now I just want to run away from the frustration and uncertainties. But I can't. I owe it to him—to our child—to figure this out. What in the world is happening between the two of us?

"Why didn't you let me know? Text? Call? Something?"

"There are rules about evidence." He knows this, too. "I can't always openly share my work with you. What I've told you this morning is already skirting the fringes of breaking those rules."

He nods. Places his own mug next to mine, and then stares directly into my eyes. "You could have let me know where you were and that you would be late. Would that be breaking the rules? Either way, you didn't. What's happening to us, Liv?"

I search his eyes for a long moment, looking for the glimpses of the man I fell in love with but all I see is anger and frustration. "I wish I knew. I can't seem to do anything right anymore. You're right, I should have called or at least sent a text but I was so upset, so confused, I couldn't think."

"I suppose Walt comforted you?"

"What?" I don't believe this. "We discussed what my father's notes could possibly mean. Trust me, it was all very clinical."

"You said yes when I asked you to marry me, Liv. You made a commitment to *me*." His tone hardens with each word. "Walt gets your days. Your nights should belong to me."

"You're twisting everything I say! Walt and I are partners—and friends. That's all. If anything, he's like a father to me."

David leans closer, stares into my eyes until I blink. "Why don't I believe you? I can't trust anything you say anymore."

The words echo in my brain as familiar as if I'd said them myself. I drown out the voices that seem to be a replay of the fight we just had. Have we had this fight before? I can't remember. The hours and days are blurring together. The headaches, the fatigue. I don't know how much more I can take. I am so, so tired. So confused. I feel completely out of control

I summon my resolve and say what needs to be said. "I honestly don't know what your deal is with Walt. It's like you're suddenly jealous of him. The idea is absurd…it's totally crazy."

He laughs. "You can't remember anything about our lives anymore and I'm the crazy one?" He flings an arm outward, toward the wall that separates the kitchen and dining room. "Your stuff still sits in boxes in the foyer. You haven't unpacked a damn one of them. Do you even want to be here, Liv?"

A distant throb starts in the back of my skull. I can't do this.

I slide from between him and the counter. "I have to get to work."

"There's the answer!" he shouts at my back. "Walk away."

I stop, turn to face him. "I'm not walking away, David. You're pushing me away."

He smiles but there is no amusement in the expression, then he bangs a fist into his chest. "I'm pushing you away? From where I'm standing, you're the one who can't wait to get away."

This time I turn my back and I keep walking.

I guess I'll just have to wait for a better time to tell him he's going to be a father.

Or maybe I won't tell him at all.

The street that leads onto the compound of Riverbend Maximum Security Institution could be the driveway to a large estate. Trees and lampposts line the long drive. Freshly cut grass spreads out for as far as the eye can see. Beyond the meticulously maintained landscape, the Cumberland River encircles the vast property. But as you round the bend in the drive you see the wire fence and the institutional boxes that make up the prison. This is no estate, no spa resort; this is a maximum security prison that houses several hundred prisoners, including the state's male death row offenders.

The sky is overcast, threatening as I climb out of the Tahoe. I draw in a deep breath heavy with the smell and taste of rain. The air crackles with the potential of the coming storm. The forecast according to the Big 98 Walt always has tuned in on his radio is rain today and possible thunderstorms late tomorrow.

I've always had a thing for thunderstorms. They make me feel alive. The crashes and booms of thunder and the steady drum of rain are soothing to my soul somehow. It's weird, I know.

"You should try talking to him again tonight."

I glance at Walt. "I will. I really don't know why he's got such a bug up his ass. Maybe he's the one having second thoughts."

Walt pauses to look at me. "If that's the case, he's a damn fool."

I refuse to tell Walt about David's jealousy where our relationship is concerned. No way would I do that to him. I will not allow David's insecurities to become Walt's guilt. Or mine, for that matter.

"Are you thinking of holding back until you see how things go from here?"

"Honestly?" I exhale a weary breath. "Yes, I am. I don't want the baby to be the only reason that we follow through with our wedding plans. If we're not supposed to do this, then we don't need to do this."

We stare at each other for a moment then carry on toward the prison entrance. What else is there to say? My relationship with David is unraveling at breakneck speed. The best I can do is brace for whatever comes next and hope we can find our way beyond this rocky place that has suddenly consumed our lives. There are so many things I should be telling him, then maybe he would understand. But I can't bring myself to do that—to expose this…*whatever it is*…that's happening to me.

Can a person have a midlife crisis at thirty?

Inside we sign in and are escorted to the warden's office. Walt informed Warden Scott Tennison what we needed when he called and made the appointment. Hopefully Tennison will have taken the time to look into his request.

Tennison is a short, heavy man who looks closer to seventy than sixty. He stands behind a government issue executive desk surrounded by government issue filing cabinets and upholstered chairs. The view out the window behind him is of the quad between buildings. There are a few trees and picnic tables, probably for staff.

Walt shakes the hand Tennison extends. "Walt Duncan," he says. "And this is my partner Olivia."

I shake the warden's hand as well. Walt left off my surname to prevent the inevitable questions of how I might be connected to the deceased psychiatrist we're here to discuss.

"Please, have a seat," Tennison says.

We settle into the stiff chairs. Tennison resumes his seat in the high back leather executive's chair—definitely not government issue.

"I had one of my assistants pull the records on Fanning's visitors," Tennison began. "Besides his attorney, he had only one during his final months with us."

The warden places four different photos across his desk, all are of my father signing in at security.

My heart thumps hard against my sternum. I ask, "There were four visits in all?"

Tennison meets my gaze. "Yes, one in December of last year, two in January of this year and then one in early February."

I struggle to conceal my surprise. "Fanning had no other visitors?" He has answered this question already, but I suddenly need confirmation that I heard right.

Tennison shrugs. "The only other person was his attorney. He visited once in January and then again one week after Dr. Newhouse's final visit."

It's not surprising that the attorney would visit considering Fanning was coming up on his release date. Why in the world would my father visit the son of a bitch four times? This makes no sense whatsoever. I wasn't aware my father even knew Fanning beyond what was seen in the news leading up to his release. If he visited him in early February it must have been only a couple of days before he died.

This is wrong somehow. My head is spinning and every breath is a struggle.

"In what capacity was Dr. Newhouse visiting Fanning?" Walt asks.

My heart practically stumbles to a stop.

"Newhouse listed himself as Fanning's therapist. I was under the impression he was helping him to prepare for being released back into society which is why I granted extended visitations."

A chill leeches into my bones. "These visits weren't recorded?" I knew the answer before I asked but I had to be sure.

"Certainly not," Tennison assures me.

"Thank you, Warden." Walt stands and thrusts out his hand.

I do the same, my knees feeling weak with this ground-shaking news. Why would my father hide this from me? We discussed Fanning's upcoming release. I remember distinctly telling him I could not believe, even with the plea deal, that his sentence wasn't at least a decade longer.

"You know," Tennison says as we prepare to go. "It's not unusual for an inmate to seek help from a therapist or a man of God prior to release. They all leave here hoping never to return. Generally, they seek counsel from one of our staff therapists. I don't know how Fanning landed himself a prestigious doctor like Newhouse."

"Maybe if we find Fanning alive, we'll learn the answer to that question," Walt replies.

I'm grateful my partner responded because I couldn't have spoken if my life depended upon it. I feel as if I'm in a dream—a nightmare—that keeps dragging me deeper and deeper into this place I don't recognize.

"The really strange part is Newhouse's last visit was quite volatile," Tennison goes on. "The guards said Fanning demanded to be taken back to his cell and that the two men were still shouting at each other when Fanning was escorted away. It didn't sound like any therapy session I've ever heard of."

Walt hesitates. "Any chance either one of those guards is on duty today?"

Air rushes into my starving lungs.

"I believe one of them is," Tennison says. "Would you want to speak with him?"

Before I can rush to say yes, Walt says, "If possible. We understand you have a prison to run here and we've already taken up a great deal of your time."

"I do have a meeting," Tennison says, "so I'll have the two of you wait in my conference room. I'll see that Officer Winslow joins you as soon as he can."

Walt and I wait in the conference room, both of us looking rattled. We know better than to discuss our concerns until we're outside these prison walls. You never know when you're being recorded, particularly since we're not attorneys or doctors.

Seven endless minutes later a tall, thin man in his mid-forties enters the room. "Ricky Winslow," he announces.

He stands at attention, awaiting our questions. My money's on him being former military. Maybe a Marine.

"Have a seat," I suggest, grateful my voice is steady once more.

Winslow pulls out the chair at the end of the table and settles into it.

Walt kicks off the questions. "Warden Tennison tells us you overheard what sounded like an argument between former inmate Joseph Fanning and Dr. Lewis Newhouse back in February."

"That's correct, sir," Winslow confirms. "We heard shouting in the interview room. Fanning's voice was particularly loud. He was calling for us. He wanted to return to his cell."

Walt appears to consider his answer for a moment. "Do you recall anything else he or Newhouse said? Think carefully," Walt urges, "this could be very important."

A frown furrows Winslow's brow as if he is doing exactly as Walt asked and concentrating hard to remember any little detail. "The doctor appeared visibly upset. I remember that. He told Fanning he'd better remember his warning or there would be severe consequences."

I swallow with effort and throw out the next question. "Did Fanning say anything in response to my—to Dr. Newhouse or to you as you escorted him back to his cell?"

Winslow shakes his head then frowns. "Wait. He kept muttering something like: *we all got bones buried somewhere.* Didn't make any sense at the time." He shrugs. "To tell you the truth, I think the man was crazy. I mean, crazier than we already knew. We all thought he got off way too light for what he did, if you know what I mean."

When I say nothing more, Walt presses, "That's all Fanning said?"

Winslow nods. "*We all got bones buried somewhere.* That's it."

The image of a shovel sliding into dirt slams into my brain with such force that I flinch.

I blink away the puzzling image. The rest of the exchange between Walt and the guard is nothing more than a jumbled hum of syllables.

This can't be—none of it. My father would never have been involved with a man like Fanning and he sure as hell didn't have any bones buried anywhere.

The sound of that shovel sliding into dirt echoes in my head again.

Nothing about any of this makes sense.

There has to be some mistake.

Poor Walt. He spent the drive from Riverbend to the next address on our list trying to reassure me that I had nothing to worry about despite what we learned from the warden and the guard. I'm a really lousy partner right now. I feel terrible that he has to deal with all these personal issues of mine on top of this perplexing case. This is not me. This is not my life. And yet, it is.

I feel like I'm coming apart from the inside out.

With every ounce of courage I possess, I focus on moving forward to the next step in the investigation. I can't look at the other for even a second longer.

Andrea Donnelly is the next name on the list of Fanning's victims. She was eleven when he picked her up from the movie theatre. An ER nurse now, Andrea is petite and pale but her voice is steady and there is strength in her eyes as she explains what happened to her nineteen years ago.

"My friends Sunny and Ellen were making fun of me because I'd told them about my secret crush on a boy in our class." She closes her eyes and shakes her head. "It was silly." Her lids flutter open once more. "They didn't mean any harm but at that age you take everything to heart. I'd gotten my period earlier than them and I guess they were jealous. God only knows why, but it was a big deal at the time."

When she hesitates I nod my understanding. "Girls can be cruel at that age."

She exhales a big breath. "I have two of my own now and I remind them every day that adolescence is the hardest time they'll face in their lives."

"You were angry with your friends so you went outside," Walt prompts.

Andrea nods. "It was so foolish. I should've stayed inside." She draws in a big breath. "But I didn't. He spotted me on the sidewalk half a block from the theatre. I was headed home. He offered me a ride. I said no, of course. But then I saw those mean boys from the high school. I was far more afraid of them than of a stranger who was old enough to be my father. And I was pretty sure I'd seen him at the the-atre dropping off his daughter, which turned out to be a mistake. Joseph Fanning never had a daughter." She shakes her head. "I don't know. I was stupid. Stupid and naive."

Andrea shares how terrified she was when she realized he wasn't taking her home and how he pulled over, yanked her out of the front seat and stuffed her into the trunk. Her throat works with the remembered fear. He took her to the rear parking lot of an abandoned factory, raped her and left her naked and unconscious on the cracked and faded pavement.

As she speaks the images flash through my mind as if I were there. I can smell the sweat from the bastard's physical exertion. Can hear his raspy panting. I can see her lying on the ground like a discarded rag doll.

The black dots float across my field of vision and I know I have to get out of this house soon or I will vomit on the woman's beautiful Persian rug.

I touch the phone at my waist and say, "I have a call."

I rush out of the house so fast I almost stumble over the dog.

DETECTIVE WALTER DUNCAN

I finish the interview as quickly as I can. Andrea Donnelly pulled a twelve-hour shift on Sunday night and spent Monday at home with a sick daughter.

There are only a few more names on the list and I am growing more convinced with each one that we're beating a dead horse. Unless Sanchez is our perp, then none of Fanning's past victims is responsible for his disappearance.

That leaves us with a family member or friend or maybe a totally unrelated vigilante.

The other option makes my heart ache. I do not want to find out that Fanning has hurt another person.

Damn him. He should have died in prison. He should be in hell where he belongs. How is it good people like my Stella can suffer such horrific, slow deaths and that bastard is still breathing?

Well, he might not still be breathing. But then again, if he is and he took a victim, that victim is likely dead by now. Dammit all to hell.

Fury quakes through me as I walk to the Tahoe. I climb behind the steering wheel and glance at my partner slumped in the passenger seat. "You okay? You don't look okay, Liv."

"I am definitely not okay." She scrubs a hand over her face. "Sorry about running out on you in there. It was either that or puke on her carpet."

"We're going to lunch. You need something in your stomach." I start the engine and pull away from the curb.

"Chances are I'll just puke it up," she says. "I can't decide if it's related to the migraines or if it's plain old morning sickness." She untwists the lid on her bottle of water and sips gingerly.

"Is that normal either way?" I am worried sick about her. If it's the migraines, that can't be good for the baby. If it's morning sickness, that can't be good for Liv. Hell, I don't know. I've never been in this situation before. My fingers tighten on the steering wheel. Damn, I wish I knew what to do.

"It can be normal either way, yeah."

She sounds so weak. "What about soup? That bread place you like has killer chicken noodle soup. You're always saying that. I'll bet soup would help."

She sighs. "Maybe. I'll give it a try."

The weight on my chest eases a little. "I kind of like that broccoli cheddar soup and I'm not usually a soup man." No one can make soup the way my Stella did. I don't have to say as much. Liv knows. Stella sent soup to her plenty of times.

"Stella spoiled you for anybody else's soup." She laughs.

I'm glad. The sound is weary but it's a laugh nonetheless. I'll take it.

I decide to lighten things up. "You been thinking about baby names?"

"Are you kidding? I'm still dealing with the concept that I'm pregnant."

I hit my blinker for the next turn. "Bullshit. Baby names have crossed your mind. That's just normal."

"Maybe I'm not normal." She smiles.

I grin. "Normal enough."

"I'll get around to names eventually."

As least she smiled and sort of laughed. That's something.

"You want to go inside and eat?"

"We probably should. That way I can make a run for the bathroom as necessary. I don't want to puke in your car."

At half past one the biggest lunch rush is over so we're served and seated fairly quickly.

"You want to talk about what the warden said?" I talked her down from the edges of hysteria as we left Riverbend. Then she moved straight to the next name on the list. I took her cue and let it ride. But Riverbend is the elephant in the room. There's no avoiding it for long.

She shrugs. "I'm thinking maybe my father spoke to Fanning on Sanchez's behalf. So far those are the only two names related to the case that I've found in my father's notes or files. Sanchez may have been his patient and he may have asked my father to talk to Fanning. It seems a bit unorthodox but there has to be some reason and that one sounds more logical than any other I can come up with. I don't believe for a second that my father was acting as Fanning's therapist. I'm certain that was a ruse to gain access to him."

"We can drop by Fanning's lawyer's office and feel him out. If Fanning had his own therapist the lawyer should have a record of the name and any visits before and after his release."

"But we both know he's not going to tell us either way."

I drink down the last of my soup, not bothering with the spoon and offer, "No harm in asking."

Liv sips at her soup for a while longer then pushes it away. She didn't eat much but at least she ate something. The few crackers she nibbled on should help as well.

Once in the Tahoe she reaches into the backseat and grabs a Walmart bag, dumps the dog shampoo out and pokes the bag into one of the cup holders in the console.

Our gazes meet. "Just in case," she explains.

The lawyer's office is on the west side of town in a sketchy strip mall. Not too far from the Reeves Accounting firm, in fact. We park in the lot and eye the two remaining businesses still operating in the strip mall. A nail salon and the lawyer's office. The other three shops are for lease. Considering the faded signs and the peeling paint they've been empty for a good long while.

She sits up straighter and asks, "We doing the good cop/bad cop routine?"

"I get to be the good cop this time," I say.

"Suits me. Right now I feel a lot more like a bad cop than a good one anyway."

I chuckle like she's joking but I have a feeling she's not kidding.

We climb out and cross the lot. The traffic on Powell is heavier than I would have expected for this time of day. There are two cars parked in front of the nail salon. One of the technicians or whatever they're called stands in the open door. She shouts a two-for-one deal at us as we move past.

Liv waves her off and goes for the lawyer's door. The door as well as the plate glass window on either side of it is covered with iron bars. There are no vehicles parked in front of this office. I imagine most of his business scurries in on foot and well after dark.

Inside, the place smells of roses, compliments of the candle burning on the receptionist's desk. The chair behind the desk is empty. She's either out to a late lunch or in her boss's office taking dictation or giving something I don't want to think about.

The sound of rain draws my gaze to the iron clad windows. A torrential downpour has started. The weatherman said it was going to rain. I guess he got it right this time. "Looks like we walked in just in time."

Liv nods. "Hopefully it'll pass before we're done here."

"Can I help you?"

The man—Alexander Cagle—is standing in the doorway of what I presume to be his office. "My secretary is at lunch." He gestures to the empty desk.

I flick the lapel of my jacket aside and reveal my badge. "Detective Walt Duncan." I hitch my head toward Liv. "My partner. Olivia. We need to ask you a few questions about a client of yours—Joseph Fanning."

Cagle's expression closes instantly. "I'm sure you know that—particularly in light of your ongoing investigation—I can't answer any of your questions, Detective."

"Your client is missing," Liv says. "If you expect us to find him, I would suggest you hear us out."

Reluctantly he leads us into his office. As soon as we're seated he picks up his cell and appears to answer a text.

While the reception area was as plain as hell with its seventies style paneling and the utilitarian tile floor like you see in hospitals, his office is as lavish as any I've encountered in the high-end law firms downtown. Mahogany desk and matching credenza. Lush carpet. Richly painted walls adorned with elegant artwork and the framed accolades that herald his right to practice law. His chair is as big as a throne and every bit as ostentatious. The two chairs flanking the front of his desk are overstuffed and clad in a classic paisley fabric.

"Sorry for the interruption, my secretary needed to confirm my order for lunch. So, what can I do to help?" He looks from me to Liv and back.

I go first. "Have you spoken with your client since his release from Riverbend?"

"I have, yes." He braces his elbows on his desk and steeples his fingers. "Of course our conversation is privileged."

Liv throws the next punch. "Did he at any time mention feeling as if he was being watched or followed?"

"He did not. In fact, he insisted he was settling in well. I can tell you that he was planning to look for part-time employment to supplement his social security."

"Have you heard from him since he disappeared?" I ask.

"I have not. If I had, I would have urged him to turn himself in so as not to waste tax payer dollars."

How nice. The two-bit, ambulance-chasing lawyer is concerned about waste in government spending. I wish I had a nickel for every sign plastered around the city with his face and stupid logo on it. Not to mention the television and radio commercials. I resist the urge to roll my eyes. The man has no class whatsoever beyond the paisley fabric he chose for these fancy chairs. Stella always loved paisley, said it was classic.

"Do you have any theories on what may have happened to him?" This from Liv.

"I believe a vigilante has taken him somewhere and murdered him. I don't think we'll ever hear from Joseph Fanning again unless his body is found."

Funny he doesn't sound torn up about it at all. I ask, "Are you speaking from firsthand knowledge about some aspect in his disappearance that we don't know about or are you simply theorizing?"

"She asked for a theory." He turns his hands up, his face smug. "I gave her what she asked for."

When Liv doesn't take her turn, I inquire, "Does Fanning have any friends or relatives who might be hiding him?"

"He has no family and certainly no friends."

Liv doesn't say a word. I stand. She does the same. "Well thank you, Mr. Cagle. I hope you'll call us if you think of anything that might help us find your client."

The attorney pushes up from his elegant chair and gives me a nod. "I certainly will. I am just as interested in finding my client as you."

I keep the chuckle to myself. Yeah right.

We're almost to the door when Liv turns around. "Mr. Cagle, did you hire on Mr. Fanning's behalf a private psychiatrist to help him with transitioning back into society?"

The flinch is almost imperceptible, but I spot it.

"He mentioned wanting one," Cagle says, "but I think he found one on his own."

She tilts her head. "I'm sure you remember the therapist's name."

Cagle shakes his head. "Actually, I don't." He reaches for a file on his desk, a cue that he's done answering questions. "I'll call if I think of anything else."

I follow Liv across the lobby. We stall at the door. The rain has stopped but two news vans are waiting outside right next to my Tahoe.

Son of a bitch. Cagle wasn't ordering lunch. He was ordering publicity.

DETECTIVE OLIVIA NEWHOUSE

"Detective Duncan!" a reporter shouts.

"Detective Duncan," another fires, "is it true you're treating Fanning's case as a potential homicide?"

"Detective Duncan, just one comment, please!" the first one entreaties.

Both women rush forward, blocking our path to Walt's Tahoe.

"No comment." Walt grabs me by the arm and starts ushering me toward the passenger side as if I'm a victim or a witness and not a cop.

I pull away from him and storm through the line of vultures on my own. I will not allow being pregnant or confused or upset or whatever the hell else is wrong with me to rule my existence.

My partner ignores the shouts and opens the driver's side door. The reporters crowd up to his door.

"You should give them something," I say. "We both know they will make it up if you don't. Or worse, take this deadbeat lawyer's word for why we were here."

"I hate this part," he grumbles as he lowers his window. "Lowery," he calls out to one of the reporters he knows fairly well. The brunette rushes forward, elbows past the blonde. "Like the chief said at the press conference earlier this week, we are treating this case like any other where foul play is potentially involved. We have nothing new to share. But we are hoping to have this case resolved very soon."

He powers up the window, blocking out more urgent questions.

"Good job," I say, eyes forward. "You sounded just like a politician, talking without actually saying anything."

He chuckles. "I believe I've just been insulted."

As the Tahoe reverses slowly out of the parking slot a body slams against my door. I jump. Walt hits the brakes.

The man whose face is plastered against my glass is another reporter. Don't know where this one came from or why the hell he would ram the door. He shouts at me through the glass. "Detective Newhouse, is it true Joseph Fanning was one of your father's patients?"

"Son of a bitch."

I hear the words Walt mutters, feel the SUV moving once more, see the reporter's mouth moving as he says more but I suddenly feel a million miles away.

Somehow still looking on yet unable to participate in what's happening around me.

As soon as Walt is clear of the reporters, he twists the steering wheel and guns the engine. We barrel out of the parking lot.

"He knew," I say. The fucking lawyer knew my father went to see Fanning. "He told that reporter."

It's not until we hit a red light and Walt stops that he speaks. "Looks like we stirred a hornet's nest. This is day four of our investigation. The chief mentioned both our names on day two. Why hasn't the lawyer said anything before now?"

Good question. "What do you know about the warden?"

The light turns green and Walt removes his foot from the brake and hits the gas. "Nothing. But I'll remedy that ASAP."

The ache in my brain is still distant but the black dots hanging around my vision warn that I may not be able to ward off the inevitable for long. I need to do everything I can before then.

"Take me to my car. I'll go out to the farm and start looking for any hidden files." Even as I say the words I do not believe any of this is possible. My father would never have kept a secret like this from me. Never. He was not that kind of man. Yet, how else can what we've learned be explained? "You talk to the warden again and keep me informed."

"I don't think that's a good idea." Walt shakes his head. "You need to take this slow and easy, Liv.

I'm really worried about how these revelations are affecting you."

This is the one thing I did not want: to be treated as if I'm incapable or weak. "I'll be at home, Walt. At the farm. I have the best security system on the market and it's where I feel the most relaxed these days."

When he still hesitates, I say, "We need to head this off before it becomes headlines. The chief will take me off the case." I don't have to say how this thing going public would seriously jack up my stress level.

"Point taken. We'll do this your way, but you're taking some food with you."

By the time I'm in my Subaru I have a six-pack of bottled water, a bag of crackers, individual cheese sticks, apples and grapes. Walt ordered me to eat while I work and to drink plenty of water. Just outside Nashville I ran through another rain shower but it had passed by the time I reached Franklin.

As I maneuver along the driveway that extends deep into the woods before hitting the clearing that is the family farm, one of the bags falls out of the seat and bottles of water roll around in the floorboard. I can't help but smile. Walt really does want to take care of me whether I like it or not. He cares about me. I think it's safe to say he loves me like a daughter. He really has been there for me, before and since my dad died. David is right about one thing: Walt is more than a partner. He's family.

I wish David could understand our relationship. This abrupt jealousy is so uncharacteristic. Despite his hurtful words this morning, I sent him a text explaining where I'd be for a few hours. I even double-checked my calendar to make sure the two of us had nothing planned. Of course, I didn't tell him what I would be looking for at the farm. I told him I was going to pack a few more boxes.

I am certain neither he nor his family would want to hear that there is a chance my father was treating a patient named Joseph Fanning. I don't want to hear it myself. Still refuse to believe it.

But I'm not a fool. He did visit the prison. He did pass himself off as Fanning's therapist. I also understand my father may have done those things as a way to cover his real reason for visiting the scumbag. He may have done those things to help his patient, Mario Sanchez. There is no other explanation.

A face-to-face interview with Sanchez is growing more and more important. With only a couple other names on the list of victims besides Sanchez, his is becoming increasingly more relevant. After Walt checks in with the warden, he will interview the next person on our list before he calls it a day. I feel guilty about not going with him but I need to do this. He agreed. Like me, he understands on some level that neither of us can explain that time is running out. Something bad is coming.

I emerge from the trees and my gaze sweeps across the open pastures where horses once grazed and trotted. I love this place. I absolutely cannot sell it. David will just have to deal with the idea.

The big horse barn sits a good distance from the house. It, too, is beautiful. Classic. From the outside, one would think the house is the typical farmhouse. Two stories. Wrap around porch on the first level. Salvaged brick foundation and classic white siding with wood storm shutters that actually work painted in a deep black. Topped with a metal roof, the house was built about fifty years ago but the architect went to great lengths to ensure it looked as if it had sat on this hillside overlooking the green pastures for centuries.

Inside is a different story. The house has plenty of original features like wide plank flooring and a massive stone fireplace that looks like something from the eighteenth century, but in the center of the house the ceilings soar to the roofline. The second floor hallway circles around this area, the railing open to the central living space below. Four bedrooms, each with an en suite bath, wreathe the upper floor. On the main level the centerpiece of the floor plan is the vast open space that includes the living room, kitchen and dining areas. On one end of the first floor is a massive library and work-out room while my parents' bedroom suite and my father's office are on the other end.

It's almost four when I park in front of the house and get out. The peace and quiet envelops me. There's a chill in the air but according to the news this cold spell is almost behind us. By tomorrow we should be back into average temperatures for May. Thunderstorms are supposed to usher in the warmer temps. I grab the bag of snacks, gather the bottles of water and head for the front door.

Inside I lock the door and reset the security system. I've never been afraid here but the last thing I want is some reporter walking in while I'm digging around in old files. Though I haven't experienced a reporter invasion, Walt has. He told me about one joining he and his wife in the backyard on a Sunday afternoon. Walt was grilling steaks. His wife was setting the table on the patio and all of a sudden a reporter from Nashville's biggest newspaper strolls around the end of the house and shouts a hello as if he'd been invited to lunch.

On top of not wanting a reporter to bully into my house, Fanning is still missing. If he had some relationship with my father, he could show up here. As much as I consider him the scum of the earth and not worth the cost of a bullet to his head to stop him, I don't want to have to deal with an Internal Affairs investigation about my father's potential involvement with the man and me shooting him.

I put the snacks away, grabbing myself a stick of cheese and a bottle of water before I head to my father's office. I sit in his chair and consider his desk. Might as well start at the top and work my way down. Putting aside my disbelief and dragging my objectivity back to front and center, I start with his calendar notebook for this year. Since he died on February 6, there's not a whole lot to look at. I find the dates the warden mentioned. All are marked with JF.

I shake my head. "What in the world were you doing, Dad?"

I round up an organizing bin, one of the stainless steel ones lining the shelves in the credenza behind his desk, and place the calendar there. Whatever I find that is relevant in some way to the investigation I'll put in the bin for Walt and me to dissect. Part of me feels guilty for looking through my father's things with the intent of finding evidence. But that's not exactly what I'm doing. My goal is to find no evidence. I need to discover that this was some sort of step taken in support of Sanchez. My father doing what he always did, being the man who saves the day.

There are no other notes on his desk. I open his laptop and scroll through the files there. My father wasn't big on electronic files. He preferred the old fashioned way so most of his files are paper. I peruse his contacts list, his sent and received emails. Nothing jumps out at me. No exchanges between him, the warden, the lowlife attorney or any other representative of Joseph Fanning.

I close the laptop and move on to the desk drawers. I find a bag of my father's favorite snack—Reese's candy. I open one and pop it in my mouth. The combination of chocolate and peanut butter is instantly soothing. A smile touches my lips as I think of all the times as a kid that I came into his office and shared a Reese's with him.

My continued search reveals no notes or business cards or anything else in the drawers that suggest collusion with the enemy in this case. I stand, stretch my back after being hunkered over the desk for so long. I stare at the row of steel five-drawer filing cabinets—the kind that are supposed to withstand the typical house fire for an extended period of time. I've fingered through the rows of file folders already. Didn't spot a single name on our list.

No matter, I walk over to the cabinets and open the top drawer on cabinet number one. Another look can't hurt. I begin with the first name on the list and go through it once more. Drawer after drawer, I drag it open and search. Nothing. Not a single one of Fanning's victims from before he went to prison. I double check for Sanchez, even check the files on either side of where Sanchez would be. Nada.

This makes no sense.

I scour the credenza and the rows of bookshelves and find the same. Not one thing. Then I go to my parents' bedroom.

"This is a true low point, Liv."

Guilt piling higher and higher on my shoulders, I search my parents' things. I go through all my father's clothes, check pockets, look under stacks of neatly folded clothes. I find a few coins and a gum wrapper but nothing else.

Finally I collapse on the carpeted floor of the massive walk in closet. I close my eyes and inhale the scent of my father. My mother's scent faded years ago. Unless I open one of the boxes with her favorite scarves folded neatly inside, then I can smell her perfume.

I miss them both so much.

That distant ache is building. I haven't seen the dots in the last hour or so but I fear they're coming. I need to finish before the headache hits. There is only one other place my father might hide files. Searching his bedroom for clues of a meeting with Fanning, the warden or the lawyer was a logical step. He might have left a card in a jacket pocket, or perhaps even a sticky note. But my father would never, ever hide files any place someone else might have easy access. Like his bedroom or the library.

No way. Any patient files would be under lock and key, which leads me to the only other place where he kept any sort of files. I walk down the hall from my parents' bedroom toward his office. I enter the laundry room across the hall from his office. The laundry room is quite large. There's a door to the portico that leads out to the detached garage and there's another door, this one hidden behind a tall cabinet. I open the double cabinet doors and step into the empty space. Before me is the steel door and keypad that lead to the panic room. I enter the code and the steel door slides away. It doesn't open out or into the room but disappears into a slot in the wall.

The panic room has its own heating and cooling system. A fresh air input of some sort. A small two-piece bathroom. The main part of the room is ten by twelve. The small bathroom and an equally small storage room stand side by side at the farthest end. There's a set of pull-down beds against one wall. The lower one works as a sofa as well as a bed. On the wall above it is a second pull down twin size bed that serves as an upper bunk. There's a small table surrounded by four narrow chairs. A refrigerator and a television. The electricity in the room is powered by thermal and solar energy. If the grid goes down, this room will operate.

Another filing cabinet stands in the storage room. This one doesn't have the typical lock. It's biometric. I place my thumb there and listen to the locks release. Inside are the most private files of the Newhouse family. The deed to the property is here. My parents' last will and testament was stored here until I retrieved it for settling the estate. Birth certificates, social security cards, passports and a handful of files related to upgrades and maintenance to the property. The six most recent tax year files. All of this I find in the top drawer.

I pull open the bottom drawer, there are only two. Inside, I find another row of files. I lower onto the floor, folding my legs into a comfortable sitting position and pull out the first file from the bottom drawer. The folder is marked only as "The Child." There is no name, just a long history of abuse and neglect about a small girl. The words, written by my father, are disturbing. I shudder and reach for the next file. As I read the name on the tab those damned black dots appear in my line of vision. My pulse trips with disbelief. I toss the file aside and move to the next one, the pain in my skull ramps up, rising to a crescendo.

Shelley Martin, Melanie Hardeman, Janie Hyatt, Dana Reeves, Mario Sanchez and a dozen others. They are all here.

Every single known victim of Joseph Fanning.

THE CHILD

The blood has stopped coming.

This makes me very happy. At least for a while. I haven't grown taller in the past few months, that makes me happy, too. He says I'm probably as tall as I'm going to get. I don't know when my real birthday is but he chose one for me. May fifth. On May fifth of that year I was fourteen, he told me.

Fourteen sounded really old. The breasts were finished growing, too, apparently. A C cup, he announced. I didn't really know what he meant, but he appeared to have adjusted to this new me.

I hadn't really but as long as he had, that was all that mattered.

Now we used a different method for getting money. I was still very good at pickpocketing. But it was harder to get close to the unsuspecting old ladies and the distracted mothers. I had to work harder to grab a few bucks here and there. We never took credit cards. Too much risk of getting caught, he claimed with all the authority of a man who had mooched off others his whole life. A lot of stores have cameras now, he'd told me. They could look back and see who used the credit card. So we stuck with cash rather than take the risk.

The new method of making money involved me pretending to be one of those ladies who haunted the street corners. It was easy, really. All I had to do was flirt with the guy and lure him into the alley where *he* would be waiting. Sometimes I worried about how hard he hit the guys, but none of them died as far as I know. We didn't have to worry about any one of them looking for us because we always went to another part of town or even to a nearby town. Never shit where you eat, he'd say.

Then I started to get sick. I felt really bad all the time. If I ate I puked it up. And I was so tired. He eyed me suspiciously but he wouldn't say why. I begged him to take me to the doctor but he refused. He said I'd live. And I did.

Pretty soon the sickness passed and I felt better. Not tired anymore. We kept running the scam on the guys who wanted to buy me for a few hours of disgusting pleasure. Until my belly started to swell like I had swallowed a ball or something. That was when things went to hell for me. He screamed and ranted and kicked at me. I cried and cried, begged him to tell me what was wrong. Finally, he told me I was pregnant. I knew what that meant: I was having a baby. But I shouldn't be pregnant I didn't have a husband or a boyfriend. All I had was him. Then I realized that he was the one who got me that way.

I had no idea how these things worked.

I stared at my belly. I had a baby growing inside me? He started to cuss and scream about the time he got drunk and forgot to use a condom. I didn't completely understand but I eventually figured out it had something to do with the stuff that came out of him when he was grunting and rutting into me.

The angrier he got, the more terrified I became. What were we going to do? How did I get it out? What did we do with it? At first he wouldn't answer me. He just stared at me as if I was a pile of dog shit in his path. Then he told me he was going to fix it. Over the next few days he forced me to drink nasty black medicine. When the only thing that accomplished was to make me shit myself to death, he punched me in the belly and beat me up worse than he ever had before.

That didn't work either.

My belly just kept growing.

Then he told me we would wait until it was ready to come out and take care of it then. The way he said this made me worry but I had no clue what I could do about it. He made all the decisions. I just did what I was told.

This was my life, my normal.

The first time I felt it moving around inside me I screamed. I was like, what the hell is that? I was afraid to ask him about it so I just waited and finally figured out it was the baby. For some reason, it made me happy. Really happy. I had never had any toys except for that ratty old bear. Now I was going to have a baby of my very own. I could play with it and take care of it. It would look at me the way I looked at him. We would be a family.

Except that isn't what happened.

When the labor pains began I thought I was dying for sure. I screamed and cried and screamed some more. He went and got this old woman who lived down the block. She claimed she had brought dozens of babies into the world. The pain went on for hours. It felt as if my body had a mind of its own and was going to pop open any second. The pressure. The need to push. I couldn't stop it. I had no control. I thought I was going to split in half for sure. All I could do was keep screaming.

Late that night it finally happened. The woman used her hands and fingers to help the baby come out. She said I was real lucky that she was able to help the baby come out without a lot of tearing and extra bleeding. I was still hurting like hell but mostly I just wanted to hold my baby. It was a boy. She cut the cord with scissors, then clamped it with a clothespin. She cleaned him up, wrapped him in a towel and handed him to me. He was the most beautiful thing I had ever seen.

No other baby had ever been as beautiful as him. And he was mine.

She told me to let him suck at my breast. It hurt like hell but I did it. Later I fell asleep. When I woke up the old woman was gone and so was my baby.

I stare at the disgusting shell of a man collapsed into a heap in the corner. Even as he sleeps his chest rises and falls with the rattle of the dying. The wound on his arm is infected. Yellow pus leaks from it. I am certain it hurts like a son of a bitch. I stand, walk over to him and kick him in the arm, ensuring the toe of my boot goes into the wound.

He awakens instantly, howls and writhes in pain.

I smile and wonder how much longer his black heart can hold out. Long enough to keep the misery going for a day or two more, I suspect. Long enough for me to block out the memories of what he did to me with the howls of his agony. I squat down and watch as he shudders and quakes and cries.

When he has calmed himself and the pain has subsided to a tolerable level, I'll kick him again.

Oh what fun we're going to have. Funny how his carefully laid plan to get back at me has backfired on him.

SATURDAY, MAY 5

DETECTIVE OLIVIA NEWHOUSE

I feel terrible not telling Walt the truth about the files I found at the farm. But I can't. Not yet. Not until I figure this out, at least to some degree, myself. As much as I adore Walt, love him really, it would be like betraying my father.

My cop instincts warn that I'm allowing emotion to get in the way of the job—of the law. But I just can't do it. Not yet. We still have another victim to interview. Not to mention Sanchez is coming back in to Nashville tomorrow. There's time to talk about the files later. Maybe Sanchez will shed new light on this puzzle.

I heard my father's name mentioned on the news this morning. The reporter apparently did a piece on the late news last night that was picked up on all the networks this morning. The chief has already called Walt. I expect a call from David any second.

Walt glances at me. "You okay, kid? You look exhausted."

I open my mouth to tell him I didn't sleep well but he reaches for his cell. I'm grateful for the reprieve. Gives me a minute to figure out what I am going to say.

By the time I flipped through all seventeen files last night my vision had blurred to the point that I could no longer read the words on the pages. The headache had consumed my ability to think, pain exploding over and over in my skull. I crawled to the lower bunk in the panic room and that's where I woke up this morning.

There was dried vomit on the floor so at some point I threw up. The bad taste in my mouth was more than sufficient evidence that it had come from me. Not that there was anyone else around, only me.

I rinsed my mouth and made a pot of coffee, then checked my cell for the first time since I went unconscious. David had called three times during the night. The problem is I left my cell in my father's office. No way could I have heard it through the foot of concrete that makes up the walls of the panic room.

I called him back this morning. He didn't answer so I left him a voicemail telling him I had worked so late packing at the farm that I'd fallen asleep and just decided to stay the night there. There was a nugget of truth in the story. With all that's happened I don't know how he and I will ever get back to each other. The gap between us widens a little more each day.

My mind goes back to the files. There was nothing there that suggested my father had done anything other than conduct background research on each of the victims. There were no notes from meetings or sessions. No conclusions. No summaries from telephone conversations. But why would he need background information on Fanning's victims? Since Sanchez's name is the only one I found in his office, I have a feeling it begins and ends with him.

Sanchez has to know what my father was doing. I refuse to believe he was gathering information for Fanning prior to his release. No way he would do that.

"That was Reynolds."

I force those dark worries away and turn to my partner. "He got the DNA results?"

Walt nodded. "Only on the B positive. The analysis confirms that it came from Fanning."

I blow out a breath. "Well, we knew that was coming. What's the hold up on the second type?"

"Just the timeline. We ordered the first test the day before the second. Those results will probably pop up in his system by tomorrow."

"That's something I guess." Not that we doubted that Fanning was one of the people who had been injured in whatever went down in his house. There wasn't enough blood at the scene to believe he'd died there but there was sufficient to conclude that he had sustained a serious injury.

Walt reaches for his cell again. I'm reasonably confident Reynolds hasn't gotten the other DNA results back already. Maybe his second look sifted something out of all that trace evidence. It never hurt to have a second look at the evidence. Even better if the second look is with fresh eyes.

"Thanks, buddy," Walt says before putting his phone away. "That was Renault."

Rob Renault is the detective working the two missing person cases we added to our list of potential trouble with Fanning. I brace for the news.

"Eldridge was found over in Knoxville with her boyfriend's sister." He brakes for a traffic light. "Simone is dead. They found her body this morning."

Not what I'd wanted to hear but not a surprise either. "Any chance her murder is connected to Fanning?"

Walt shakes his head. "They got the killer. The old janitor who used to work at the school. He'd been watching her for months. Bastard finally worked up the nerve to go after her. I guess he had too much time on his hands after he retired."

I close my eyes and shake my head. "Sick fuck."

"My thoughts exactly."

I can only imagine what the Simones are going through. How in the world can a sane person bring a child into this screwed up world? I think of the child developing inside me and I wonder if I'm making the mistake of my life. Will he or she blame me for dragging him or her into this shitty place?

Too late to worry about that now. It's done.

Walt parks a few yards from the front of Melanie Hardeman's home. It's a modest brick on Second

Street in Cleveland Park. The neighborhood is up and coming. Lots of hipsters moving in, jazzing things up. Melanie is my age, thirty. She's a beautician. Single. No kids.

I scan the street as we wander up the walk to the front door. A newspaper lies on the small porch. Since there's no garage and no driveway, street parking only, I'm thinking Hardeman uses the front door. With the newspaper untouched it's possible she isn't home. Her car certainly isn't anywhere near the house. The shop where she works said she was off today. Maybe she's visiting a friend or shopping.

Walt knocks on the door.

No television or other sounds beyond the closed door. Blinds are shut tight so there's no looking in through the windows.

"Looks like we'll have to give the lady a call."

There's a good chance once she learns what we want that she'll blow us off. All too often victims don't want to talk about what happened. It's too painful, too humiliating. I can understand how they feel. At this point reliving the nightmare won't change anything about what happened to them. But it's our job to convince them that their nightmare might prevent the same thing from happening to someone else.

Walt reaches for his phone at the same time a silver Impala pulls to the curb in front of the house. I elbow him and nod toward the street. A woman, tall, brunette, dressed in leggings and a long tee, emerges from the Impala. Shopping bag in her arms, she is around the hood and headed up the walk before she looks up and spots us.

I smile.

Walt says, "Good morning, Ms. Hardeman. I'm Detective—"

The bag hits the ground and Hardeman runs.

"Well shit," Walt grumbles.

I take off, dodging the apples and oranges rolling across the sidewalk.

Walt is right behind me.

"Ms. Hardeman," I shout, "we only have a few questions for you. You are not in any kind of trouble."

She keeps running.

We didn't find a criminal record. What's up with this reaction to a visit from the cops? Drugs are the first things that come to mind. Maybe there's a hit of her drug of choice in that bag back there.

My heart is pounding as I grow closer and closer to her. The woman clearly runs regularly. I have been ignoring my workout routine lately and it shows.

Just as I draw within reach of her she apparently runs out of steam and slows to a stop.

We both bend over and struggle to catch our breath.

"You're not in trouble," I repeat between gasps for air.

Walt trudges up to where we are huddled. "No offense, ma'am," he complains between gasps, "what the hell was that about?"

"I did it, okay?"

Walt and I exchange a look then stare at her. Is the woman admitting that she kidnapped Joseph Fanning?

"What did you do, Ms. Hardeman?" I ask.

She flops down on her butt on the ground, puts her knees up and wraps her arms them. "I found out where he lived and I watched him. I followed him around. Harassed him in the supermarket. I know I shouldn't have, but I couldn't help it."

"At any time did you touch him?" Walt asks, his voice still breathy.

"I didn't lay a hand on that son of a bitch. I just heckled him. I made sure that the customers at every store he went into knew what he was. I followed him through each department, shouting to all who would listen until he left the store empty handed. I hoped he would starve to death."

It's hard to shame a woman for heckling the man who raped her as a child. "Did he ever speak to you?" I ask.

Walt goes down on one knee, his forearm braced on his thigh. He's obviously struggling to catch his breath. His face is pale, beads of sweat slip down his forehead. I drop into a crouch as if to catch my breath as well, but mostly I just want to be at his level so I can better assess his condition.

"He wouldn't even look at me," Hardeman says, drawing my attention back to her. "No matter how often I showed up, he tried to ignore me. He pushed his cart around, reaching for whatever was on his list. Eventually he couldn't take it anymore and he abandoned his cart and left. I never followed him outside. I wasn't quite that brave."

"Did you ever see him with anyone?"

She shakes her head at Walt's question. "He was always alone."

"Did you notice anyone else following him or watching him?" Walt scrubs a hand over his face. If possible it's even whiter than it was before.

I start to ask him if he's okay but figure I better wait until we're finished here. Men don't like to have their weaknesses pointed out. Not even smart guys like Walt.

Hardeman appears to consider his question. "I can't remember anyone, but I was always so angry and focused on him that I can't be sure I was really looking either."

"Did he ever show up at your house?" I ask. "Try to turn the tables on you?"

She shakes her head. "I thought about that later, after I'd already harassed him a couple of times. But thank God he never came around."

"Are you certain he recognized you?" Walt asks.

Good point. If he thought she was someone else, he might have gone after the wrong person. This whole thing may have started with Hardeman's heckling.

"I told him who I was." She raises her chin in defiance. "I wanted him to know I was no longer afraid of him."

I stand, offer her my hand. "Thank you, Ms. Hardeman. We'll be in touch if we think of any other questions."

She pulls up, dusts off her bottom. "Sorry I ran. I guess I got scared and panicked."

I offer Walt my hand but he waves me off and pops up like a man half his age. He reaches into his pocket for a business card and hands it to Hardeman. "Sorry we scared you." He chuckles and swabs at his face again. "The way you ran we were worried you had a kilo of blow or something in that bag of yours."

Hardeman's expression freezes.

Oh hell.

She shrugs. "It's only a gram."

DETECTIVE WALTER DUNCAN

Sometimes as a cop the best thing to do is walk away. Since Hardeman was never arrested before, never been in any kind of trouble, we let the whole confession go. We didn't see the drugs. We had no reason to search her bag of groceries or her car. We came to ask her questions about Fanning and she answered those.

End of story.

We're three blocks away from the woman's house when the coughing starts.

I try to get it under control but the spasms won't stop. The pain shears through my body, twists inside me like barbed wire.

I can't catch my breath.

"Walt, you okay?"

I whip over to the curb, push the gearshift into Park and shove open the door.

I'm on my hands and knees on the pavement when Liv reaches me.

"Can you breathe?"

I nod jerkily, dragging in a short breath before I start coughing again.

"Should I call 911?"

I grab her arm with one hand and shake my head. Tears and snot flow down my face as I try to regain control of my respiratory system. The coughing gets nastier for a half a minute. Son of a bitch, this is the worst one yet. I hack and hack and hack until I feel like my lungs will burst out through my throat.

Liv hovers next to me, her face cluttered with worry and fear.

Finally, things start to calm down to a mere wheeze. I sit back on my heels.

"Let me get you some water."

She dashes away. I fumble in my pocket for a handkerchief and swab at my face. My chest heaves but the air just won't come in fast enough. My heart thuds wildly, trying hard to push enough oxygenated blood through my veins.

As the coughing spasms subside, the pain gets worse. Sharp, jagged shards of searing pain fire through me.

My hand shaking, I shove the handkerchief back into my pocket and dig for the small vial of pain pills. I try to open it. Can't. The damned pharmacy put a childproof top on the damned thing. I've never had a childproof top before! Why start now? Goddammit!

"Let me try." Liv takes the vial of pills from my hand and places the water bottle there in its place.

The top is already off the bottle of water so I sip it slowly, let it soothe my raw throat. This is by far the worst coughing jag I've had. The pain is excruciating. My whole body shakes with the tension of holding back the howls of agony.

Liv doesn't read the label on the vial. She simply opens it. "One or two?"

"Two." I spit the word.

I've only taken two when I'm at home. The pain roars, reminding who is master. I need two. My hands are shaking, the water sloshing in the bottle.

"Open your mouth."

I don't argue. I comply. She pops the pills into my mouth and I swallow. Follow with a swig of water. My eyes close in blessed hope. It takes a few minutes, maybe twenty, but relief will come.

"I'm taking you one of two places," she says firmly. "To your doctor's office or the ER. Which will it be?"

"Home." I grab my open vehicle door and pull myself up. My body trembles. "There's nothing the doctor or the ER can do for me."

Her face says she needs an explanation. I shake my head. "I just need to get home. I'll tell you everything then."

"Can you drive?"

"Better not," I confess.

She doesn't attempt to lead me like a crippled old man. Instead she walks next to me all the way around the vehicle, opens the passenger side door and waits for me to climb inside. Once I'm seated, she closes the door and returns to the driver's side.

While she climbs in and adjusts the seat, I shove the bottle of water into a cup holder in the console and fidget with my seatbelt. I can breathe fairly easily now. The pain spike is leveling off, not gone by a long shot but not worsening.

Liv puts the Tahoe in Drive and rolls away from the curb. I sit in silence and wait for her questions. I'm dying. I don't want to talk about that reality but I'm confident there will be no escaping the coming interrogation.

"You want to talk about it?"

"Nope."

"Okay."

She drives. I slump in the seat waiting for the painkillers to kick in fully.

The car stops and I open my eyes to mere slits. They feel too heavy to open wider and besides, pushing the issue might banish the fog I've drifted into.

The pain is floating around me. It's still there but it can't touch me through the haze of medication.

"I'll be right back," she says.

Through the narrow slits I watch Liv go to the front door, unlock it and push it open. Sandy rushes out to greet her, then follows her back to my side of the Tahoe. I try to unfasten my seatbelt but my hands aren't working so well. Liv opens the door, steps up on the running board and reaches across me to unfasten the damn thing.

"Take it slow," she says as she steps away.

Sandy dances from side to side. Even she looks worried about me. Probably remembering me bringing Stella home looking like this.

I practically fall out again, this time Liv keeps me from hitting the ground. She leads me away from the door, shoves it closed with her hip and then guides me to the house. Sandy sniffs at my right hand where it dangles at my side. I scrub at her head and make soothing sounds.

Liv doesn't stop in the living room, she takes me straight through to my bedroom. She visited Stella there once. Liv and I had just started to work together when Stella was diagnosed. My former partner was still working then. He put off his retirement until I was able to come back to work full-time. Before that, whenever I was able to come in for a few hours, he, Liv and I worked together.

I wonder who will be Liv's partner when I'm gone.

I sit on the side of the bed, shoulders slumped forward as she kneels before me and tugs off my boots.

"I can do that," I say, my tongue thick. Oh hell. I sound like a drunk.

"You just take it easy," she says as one boot pulls free. "I got this."

Once my boots are off, she peels away my jacket next. I hear the rattle of pills as she places the small vial on the table next to the bed. She removes my side arm and clip as well as my badge, places both next to the pain meds.

She urges me to lie back, then lifts my legs onto the bed. She covers me with the big old afghan at the foot of the bed. Stella made that afghan a million years ago. It has lain draped across the foot of our bed for as long as I can remember.

Stella. I wish she were here. I blink back the damn emotion. No. That's not right. I wouldn't wish this on anyone. The yearning to have someone with me for what's coming is just selfish.

I hear the water running in the bathroom that connects to our bedroom. Liv brings a glass of water and places it on the bedside table, then perches on the edge of the bed next to me. For a long time she just sits there, holding my hand. I close my eyes. Can't ignore the pull of the drugs. The pain has vanished now.

"Tell me what's going on, Walt."

Her words nudge my eyes open a crack. I lick my lips.

"You want a drink of water?"

"Nah." I drag in a big breath, thankful my lungs are working properly again. "I'm dying, Liv."

"Sick of me as a partner already, are you?"

I hear the teasing quality in her voice but I also hear the uncertainty. "It's not you, kid. It's those damn Pall Malls I smoked for half my life. Dumbest thing I ever did."

Her soft fingers tighten on my hand. "What're you doing about it?"

"Nothing I can do," I lie. "Terminal. Got three months max."

"What about chemo or—"

"Not after what I watched it do to Stella. No point. I'm dying anyway. Why make my last days suck for no good reason?"

She wants to argue with me. I can tell. But she doesn't. I feel those soft fingers trembling now. Well, hell. I didn't want to put her through this. She has enough going on in her life.

"I've taken care of most everything," I say. "My final arrangements, the house. I just don't know what to do with Sandy. I want to make sure she ends up in a good home."

"I'll take her." Liv's fingers tighten firmly on mine. "You don't worry about Sandy. I'll take good care of her and love her just the same as you do. You have my word."

"Are you sure? Preston might not want a dog?"

"Tough." She shrugs. "The truth is I'm thinking about moving back to the farm. I'm not so sure David and I were meant to be."

I frown. "What about the baby?"

She shrugs again. "I don't know. I haven't gotten to that yet."

"You'll figure it out." I reach up and tug at a wisp of hair that's fallen loose from her ponytail. "You're good people, Liv. Preston is good people, I think. Maybe." I feel my lips grinning. "Probably. You should give him another chance. I don't want you to be alone. It sucks."

She laughs, but the smile slips and the sound fades away. "My father was investigating Fanning or digging around in his past. It's far more than his visits to Fanning in prison."

I wait for her to go on. She won't look at me for a time. I get it. Whatever she's discovered is confusing, maybe even disappointing.

"I found a file on each of the seventeen Fanning victims." She exhales a big breath. "They were hidden in the panic room in the cabinet where he kept the personal files, like the deed to the farm and stuff like that." She swipes back a tear from one cheek. "I don't understand it. He never mentioned Fanning or anything about his victims."

"Are they case files? Was he treating any of them?" Seems like that's what she's saying but I don't know how one of them wouldn't have mentioned having seen a shrink with the same name as the detective doing the questioning. Doesn't make a whole lot of sense.

"I don't think he was treating them, at least not anyone but Sanchez. The files are more like background information taken from various sources. I don't understand why he would have wanted this information unless he gathered it for Sanchez or, worst case, for Fanning. That's the part that really worries me. I can't believe he would do that."

"You're worried he was working for Fanning?"

Another big breath heaves out of her weary body. "Yeah. I don't want to believe it, but there was obviously something going on that involved Fanning."

"But maybe not in the way you think," I counter. "Whatever Dr. Newhouse was doing, it wasn't to help a man like Fanning. We both know better than that. The only way he would have been working with a piece of shit like that was if the court ordered him to and since he was retired you know that can't be the case. Like I told the chief, we don't know what any of this means yet."

She nods, some of the worry disappearing. "You're right. It would just be nice to understand, the sooner the better."

"Sanchez will be back tomorrow. Maybe he can tell us what was going on." I squeeze her hand. "Go home. Get some rest. I'll be as good as new tomorrow. I promise."

"No way, partner. I'm staying until I know you're good for the night then I'll get a cab back to my car."

I'd argue but Liv is as hardheaded as I am. "Fine. Then make yourself useful and feed Sandy."

Sandy barks as if she knows exactly what I said.

I watch her prance out of the room at Liv's side.

Now I can die in peace. Sandy will be okay.

That damn frown nags at my forehead again.

But what about Liv? Will she be okay?

THE CHILD

I have no idea how many months passed with me in a daze. I didn't care if I lived or died. I thought of my baby all the time. I begged him to tell me what he'd done with him, but he just laughed at me.

I made up my mind then and there that he would never hurt me again. I was no longer going to allow him to rule my world. I was old enough to begin to see that I didn't need him to survive anymore. I could take care of myself.

The way I saw it, the biggest drawback to my situation was the fact that I couldn't read. Couldn't write. Didn't understand math. I was illiterate. But he always refused to teach me to read. No way was he going to teach me to write and to do math. I wasn't entirely sure he could do either of those things very well himself.

So I bided my time. There always times when he disappeared for a few hours. I had no idea what he was doing since he refused to include me anymore. Since he had stopped rutting into me very often I figured he might be out finding other girls to stick his nasty thing into. The idea made me jealous a little. I belonged to him. He was my family. Then I thought of the baby and I knew all that I had believed was a lie.

He was not my family. I did not belong to him. I belonged to *me*. The baby was the only real family I would ever have and he was gone.

The next time he went out for a while, I sneaked to a neighbor's house. She wasn't the old lady who helped get the baby out of me, she had moved away. This one was a younger woman. She worked a street corner. I had seen her a couple of times back when we used to pretend I was one of those girls to fool old men and get their money. But I didn't care what she was as long as she could read and write, that was all that mattered.

When I asked her to teach me to read she laughed. She thought I was kidding. "You can't read? What the hell? You some kinda retard?"

Angry tears burned my eyes but I refused to cry. "No one ever taught me," I snarled. "I've never been to school."

The look on her face told me she suddenly felt bad about what she said. When she agreed to teach me, I made her promise never to tell him. We had to do it in secret. She seemed to like that part most of all. We agreed she would call me girl since I didn't know my name. I didn't want her to call me it.

Learning was slow at first and I started to think maybe I was a retard. But then the words began to click in my brain. The letters and the sounds they made when put together fused in my memory. Pretty soon I could read. I have never been so happy about anything in my life except for those few minutes when I held my baby.

Writing was harder, but I got it. My handwriting was really pathetic, but I could do it. When I had a good handle on the reading and the writing, she started with the basic math concepts: addition and subtraction. Then she made me memorize the multiplication table. She said her mother had made her do that when she was a kid. Once I knew the multiplication table by heart she taught me about division.

One day she looked at me and said she'd never realized how much she'd taken for granted her whole life. She'd learned all this stuff as a little kid. Everyone she knew had learned it. To run into someone so young like me who hadn't had the opportunity, who couldn't read or write or do math in this day and time, was just weird, she'd said.

It was weird. I was weird.

I realized for the first time since I was seven years old that he was not my father or mother or family or friend. He became my whole world because I was his prisoner for all those years. I hadn't understood that profound fact because I never had a real family. I had no idea what one was supposed to be like. Think about when someone asks you to describe what chocolate tastes like or what closing your eyes and spinning around and around feels like, telling them should be easy, right? But if you've never tasted chocolate or never spun around, it's not so easy.

At that moment I realized that I might never know what it felt like to have a real family, but I was going to make sure I was smart and strong and that I could take care of myself. No one—especially not him—would ever hurt or control me again.

That was the day I stopped being his *it*.

DETECTIVE OLIVIA NEWHOUSE

A nightmare wakes me.

I sit straight up in the bed, struggle to gain my bearings. The darkness crushes against me. I take a deep breath. Remind myself to breath slow and deep. Thunder booms and a streak of lightning flashes, brightening the darkness for an instant. Rain beats against the roof. What the hell was I dreaming? Something about that child I read about in my father's file. Jesus. I shudder.

David sleeps soundly next to me. The soft rumble of his snoring should be comforting but it makes me shiver again, reminds me of the nightmare.

What the hell was the dream about, anyway? Beyond the girl in the file, I mean.

I can't remember the details, only snippets. Fear...running. She was lost and then the dream was suddenly about me and I was in my father's arms. My father morphed into Walt.

Walt.

Jesus Christ. Walt is dying.

Tears flood my eyes and rush down my cheeks. How can I lose him, too?

I push back the covers and climb out of the bed, careful not to wake David. Dinner was awkward. He barely said a dozen words. I rattled on about all the packing I had done at the farm. I promised to unpack the boxes I'd already brought to his house within the next few days. I assured him the news reports about my father were twisted and blown out of proportion. Mostly I lied with every breath, saying the things I knew he wanted to hear.

What I didn't do was tell him about the pregnancy...the baby.

I slip from the room and move more quickly along the hall, down the stairs and into the kitchen. I need something to help me sleep. What I would give for a couple of beers. Can't go there. Can't have a sleeping pill. I have a few of those left over from when my father died. I think I even have a couple of Valium. Can't go there either.

My heart still thuds in my chest. The snippets of images and sounds from the nightmare keep haunting me. I need to do something to wear off all the adrenaline. Wear myself out so I can go back to sleep. Walt needs me to be strong, to take the lead if necessary. I'm his partner. He's counting on me. I need to be at my best in the morning.

I pad into the entry hall and stare at the boxes. I guess unpacking a few things is as good a way as any to burn off stress. Or I could just go out and take a nice, long run in the rain—except it's not just raining, it's storming. A boom crashes outside as if to confirm my assessment. I like storms, but not running in them. I have no desire to test Mother Nature.

Unpacking it is.

I pick up the knife I left here the other night. A memory flashes—something sharp jabbing into my upper arm. Pain spears me. I frown. I pull up the short sleeve on my left arm and look. Nothing. But then my skin on the underside seems to burn. I toss the knife aside, walk to the mirror above the hall table near the front door and raise my arm so that I can see the backside—the part I can't see no matter how I twist my head around unless I have a mirror.

I stare at the small gash. It's healing. Looks days old. How the hell could I have done that and not remember? I should have felt it every time I took a shower. It's a miracle it didn't get infected. Damn. Memories of a cardboard flap slicing my arm, me rushing for something to staunch the flow pour into my mind. I walk back to the stack of boxes and lift the flaps of the one I have opened. Sure enough blood stains one of the corners. How in the world could I have done that and not remember? I don't even remember opening this damned box.

I shake off the suddenly very real idea that I'm losing my mind and force my attention to the task at hand. I pick up the knife and cut the tape over the flaps on another box. As I draw the flaps open I think of the one file I didn't tell Walt about. I really should have told him.

But something about it scared the hell out of me. I can't quite label the feelings. Between that damned file and Walt's news, I came home a mess. Holding it together through dinner must have prompted the nightmare.

Last night, after I'd sifted through the files on Fanning's victims, I moved back to the one labeled: "The Child." The patient was obviously female and she was my father's patient. The notes weren't like the usual office visit notes. These were more like notes made on visits to the patient in some sort of facility. Observations. Hypnosis therapy. Maybe the patient was in the hospital or a mental health facility.

I just need to know what my father was doing and why the files were separate from the rest of his patient files.

Unable to think about all the questions anymore, I pull a framed photograph from the box I've opened. My graduation from the police academy. I smile at the photo of my parents and me. It was the last time we were all together before my mother died. I slide my finger across the glass as if I can touch their smiling faces. It was a really happy day.

I think of my childhood growing up on the farm. I was so protected. Even as a teenager. My parents took such good care of me. Then I think of the child in that file and how horrible her childhood was.

My father's notes detailed the neglect she suffered at the hands of her biological parents. The mother overdosed when the girl was only seven.

Things grew worse from there. The father was help-less. When it became obvious he couldn't take care of himself much less the child, he sold her to a man for money to buy drugs.

How could any father do such a thing?

But it happens and, as a cop, I know this better than most.

The truly bizarre part of the child's story was the shocking detail about to whom the father sold her: Joseph Fanning. There is nothing in the case files about Fanning having a young girl with him at any time beyond his catch and release victims. I replay the interview with Andrea Donnelly. She remem-bered thinking she saw Fanning drop off a girl at the theatre. At the time, she had thought the girl was his daughter, which made her less afraid of him. The idea was dismissed since no other victim mentioned having seen anyone with Fanning.

Then again, he moved around Davidson County like a gypsy, never straying too far from Nashville and never staying in one place too long. When questioning neighbors in the few places the original detectives investigating the case knew to look, they discovered very little cooperation. No one wanted to get involved. If they dared to talk about what a neighbor had been doing perhaps his or her own secrets would be revealed. See no evil, hear no evil, speak no evil. People who live that kind of life have their own rules and those rules rarely line up with the law. Fear is a powerful motivator.

Nothing in any case files related to Fanning suggest he kept a victim. My gut clenches at the memory of reading the depraved things he did to that poor girl.

There is no description of the child, only references to she and her. At the time of my father's interviews she appeared to be about fifteen. She wasn't sure of her actual birth date. She couldn't remember the names of her bio parents.

The final entry in the file states the child died.

It doesn't say where she died. I have no idea how my father even knew her or came to have her as a patient. Logic suggests that she was a patient at one of the mental health facilities around Nashville. But her file as well as the others who were victims of Fanning being among my father's personal files makes no sense.

How are those victims connected to Dr. Lewis Newhouse?

A jab of pain spears so sharply and deeply into my brain that I grab the box to keep myself steady. The framed photograph from my graduation slips between my body and the boxes and bumps to the floor. Thankfully, no shattering of glass.

I take a breath, squeeze my eyes shut to ride out the wave of pain. What the hell is happening to me? How many headaches does this make this week? Half a dozen? Somehow I manage to pick up the photograph and place it back into the box.

The faces in the photo blur and other images tumble one over the other through my mind. Me stumbling near the edge of the woods. The smell of freshly turned earth fills my nostrils, expands in my lungs. A mound near a copse of trees. A *grave*. Someone buried in the woods.

She is gone forever now, Liv. At peace. My father's voice whispers those words to me.

I think of my mother. But wait, we didn't bury my mother at the farm. I think of the prison guard and how he said that Fanning kept muttering the same thing over and over after the angry scene at the prison with my father.

…we all got bones buried somewhere.

The sound of a shovel sliding into soil cracks through my brain. The pain that follows brings me to my knees.

She's never coming back, Liv.

SUNDAY, MAY 6

DETECTIVE OLIVIA NEWHOUSE

Someone is screaming.

I feel myself drifting through the fog of sleep, rushing toward the sound. I need to wake up. He's calling my name. *Liv! Liv! What the hell happened?*

My eyes open.

Sunlight filters in through the plantation shutters. It's so bright. I close my eyes again.

"Liv!"

Hands grip my shoulders and shake me.

I open my eyes again. David is staring at me, his expression clouded with fear, his eyes wide in uncertainty.

Walt. What if something has happened to Walt?

Air rushes into my lungs as if I have only now started to breathe. I sit up. "What happened?"

David blinks, stares at me as if I've lost my mind.

"What happened?" he echoes. "That's what I want to know." He waves a hand at the bed. "Where the hell did all that mud come from? I've been all around the house and I can't figure out where this came from. Your shoes are on the side porch caked in mud. The floorboard in your Subaru is smeared with mud. Did this happen at a crime scene? What time did you leave the house?"

As the questions fire from his lips my gaze travels down the length of me. He has pulled the covers back and he's right, I am covered in mud from the waist down. My jeans are caked with it. My socks are muddy. I stare at my hands; they are muddy as well as bloody.

Blood? Shit. Where did the blood come from?

"Tell me what's going on, Liv?"

I meet his gaze. "I was called to a crime scene. It was storming." I blink to hide the lie in my eyes. "A headache started on my way home. By the time I got here I was out of my mind in pain. I must have come straight upstairs and climbed into the bed. I'm sorry." I look at the mess I've made. "I'll clean it up."

"Just stop." He waves his hands back and forth. "The housekeeper will take care of it. It's you I'm worried about."

"Don't be ridiculous, David," I argue as I sit up. The room spins. "I'm fine."

He shakes his head and walks away.

My heart sinks and my stomach lurches. I stumble from the soiled linens and rush to the bathroom. There's nothing in my stomach to evacuate beyond the bitter bile that coats my throat and mouth on its way up and out. I sit on the Italian tile floor, the cold leeching into my bones.

Finally, when I have heaved until I feel like my eyeballs will pop out of my head, the urge fades and I drag myself to the shower and turn on the water. Feeling like death, I peel off my filthy clothes and climb beneath the hot spray, allow the heat and pressure to cleanse my skin, to warm the muscles and bones beneath. My palms burn as if I've poured alcohol onto an open wound. I turn my hands up and stare. The skin is raw and red, what looks like ruptured blisters seep blood.

The shovel. The words penetrate the cloud of disbelief still banked around my brain and images pour in. Digging. Rain pouring down on me. My hair plastered to my head. My hands burning as I keep driving the shovel into the ground.

A flash of lightning reveals the barn in the distance.

The farm. I was at the farm…*digging?*

Did I bury the files? Try to hide my father's connection to Fanning?

I shut off the water and grab a towel. As fast as I can I scrub the high-end terry cloth over my skin and rush to the closet. Jeans, sweat shirt, socks and sneakers. I run a comb through my hair. I should dry it but I don't care. There's no time for that. I grab my badge and service weapon from the bedside table. No phone. I glance around the floor. I check beneath the tousled covers. Nope. Dammit.

Taking the stairs two at a time I try to think where my cell phone is. What about my wallet? I'm not big on purses so when I'm on duty I just carry a small credit card style wallet with my license and pertinent plastic. Anything else I need I stick in my jacket pocket.

I would rather avoid the kitchen since David is apparently in there but my keys aren't in the entry hall and he said I left my muddy shoes on the side porch. My keys are likely on the kitchen counter.

I push my wet hair from my face. Water from the ends seeps into the cotton of my sweatshirt.

"Coffee?" He lifts his cup as I enter the room.

"No time." I walk straight to the counter by the side door and reach for my keys.

"You're really just going to leave."

I close my eyes and wish for a way to explain but there is no way. I have no idea what's happening to me. How am I supposed to explain it to him?

"We'll talk when I get home," I promise the same way I've promised a dozen times before. Just this week I've made that promise several times.

He moves up behind me and I shiver with the urge to run. He has no idea that I am falling apart— unraveling at the seams—and I don't know why. I only know that I have to go and find out what I was digging up last night. *Or burying.*

My mother is buried at Woodlawn in the same family plot as her parents and her brother who died as a small boy. My father was buried next to her just a few months ago. There can't possibly be anyone buried at the farm.

"Is this the end of us, Liv? Are we over? Maybe you just don't know how to tell me you don't want me anymore."

I turn to him, can't leave him feeling this way. "It isn't you, David." I stare up into his eyes and tell him as much of the truth as I can...as I understand. "Something is wrong with me. Something I can't comprehend. These headaches are coming with bizarre flashes of memory and I don't know what any of it means. I have to figure this out before I can do anything else, do you understand?"

Maybe it was the sheer agony in my voice or the fear in my eyes but he nods. Then his lips tighten. "Is Walt helping you figure it out?"

I want to scream at him. Instead I tell him the truth. "No. None of this is about Walt or about you. It's about me and something about my past that I can't remember."

Fury flashes in his dark eyes. "Don't expect me to believe you haven't told *him*."

Enough. "You need to stop blaming every issue we have on Walt. This isn't about him. He doesn't know what happened last night. He doesn't know about the memories. He doesn't know any of this." And he doesn't. He knows about my worries where my father's files are concerned, but he doesn't know the rest.

"So there was no crime scene last night?" David accuses. "That was a lie."

I hold up my hands, try to calm myself before I speak. "It's difficult to explain."

"I can't trust anything you tell me anymore. I'm sure Walt knows all about whatever the hell this is. He's the one you always turn to!" David throws his arms up. "You never come to me with your worries about work or my family or anything. I'm sick of standing in his shadow."

At that moment I don't know what comes over me but I can't take anymore and the words burst out of me. "Walt is dying, David. Get off my back about Walt."

Then I do what I should have done minutes before. I walk out the door.

My cell phone and my wallet are in my car. The cell phone is dead so I plug it in and drive away from the man who will thank me when this—whatever the hell it is—is over. No matter that I have no idea what any of this means, I understand with utter certainty that David is far better off without me.

The blisters on my palms burning, I grip the steering wheel more tightly and barrel out onto the street.

I drive like a bat out of hell. The sooner I get to the farm, the sooner I'll know what really happened last night.

Half an hour later I park in front of the house. The front door stands wide open.

My heart drums in my chest.

I swallow, wish I had some water.

I climb out of the car and walk toward the porch. My fingers curl around the butt of my weapon. Without making a sound I climb the steps. The breeze whispers in my ears, I tune out the sound.

Slowly I move across the porch and into the house. Total silence. Room by room, I go through the downstairs. All is clear, the safe room is just as I left it with the dried vomit on the floor and files spread around like discarded life stories.

I check the library and that side of the house, then slowly climb the stairs. I go through the four rooms, including the one that was mine until recently. No one. Nothing.

The house is clear. I must have left the front door open.

Deep breath. I descend the stairs and walk back outside. The sun is warm and so bright it hurts my eyes.

There's no mud on the porch so I left the house open before I got muddy. Did I see something in the files that made me believe something was buried on the property? Other files my father wanted to hide? Information about Fanning?

Or was I the one doing the burying? It's possible that during some sort of crazy blackout I decided I needed to protect him.

My body starts to shake and I feel sick to my stomach. My gaze rests on the barn. I start in that direction but then I notice the shed door is standing open. Behind the house there is the detached garage and a few yards away is a small garden shed that belonged to my mother. It was her haven. Her gardening tools and fertilizers are still stored there.

Did I go in there? My heart thumps.

I walk toward the shed with the sensation that I am watching myself do this. It feels surreal. Not me. This can't be me. Can't be my life. The closer I come to the shed, the more certain I am that I cannot go inside.

No choice.

I rest my hand on the butt of my weapon and I step inside. The interior is shaded from the sun, it's dark and cool inside. I reach up and pull the string. A single bare bulb blares to life overhead.

No mud. Nothing appears out of place. My gaze darts around the room. It's only about twelve by fifteen feet with a nice long worktable in the center. Shelves line three of the walls. Tools hang from pegboard along the fourth wall.

My gaze settles on a pale shadow on the pegboard. The place where a shovel once hung. My gut tightens.

Okay. There was a shovel. Apparently I did do some digging. My palms burn, reminding me that there was never really any question. I walk back outside and wander around the yard, widening my search for a chunk of mud or some muddy tracks. If I dug something up and then walked back to my car, based on the mud on my shoes and jeans, I had to leave a trail.

I see a blob of mud in the grass. Then another and another. I follow the random trail until the mud splotches become bigger, closer together. The path leads me to the tree line and then disappears into the thick undergrowth.

I have to look carefully to find the broken sprigs of greenery, the bent limbs of wild shrubs, but I locate the path once more. As I wade through the brush, my clothes getting damp from the moisture clinging to the leaves, I see where larger limbs have been broken from bushes and small saplings. I couldn't have wreaked that much havoc just walking or running past. I inspect a fractured limb. This was broken off at my shoulder level. Why would I feel the need to tear off limbs and sprigs of shrubs?

I must have totally lost my mind.

Fear knots in my belly. I am, I decide, slipping over some edge that I cannot see.

About twenty yards into the woods I find a small clearing. The missing shovel lies on a mound of dirt that has been exhumed from the center of the clearing. At the head of the open hole is a rusty metal cross that has obviously been here for some time. My knees threaten to give out on me.

The hole in the ground takes up most of the cleared space next to the mound of dirt. The shape is undeniably the proper size for burying a body.

I shake my head. This cannot be. But the cross—my gaze touches the rusty metal again. My heart thumps harder and harder and I can't breathe.

I stare into the hole where the missing tree limbs and sprigs of brush line the bottom. My next breath is a struggle. "Just get it over with," I mutter.

Holding onto a sapling, I ease down into the waist deep pit. Whatever else happens, I have to know what I put in this fucking hole…or whatever was already here. I reach for the limbs, toss first one and then another out of the way.

I remove another handful and there, on the ground, in front of me are bones. A skeleton. It appears to have been wrapped in a pink blanket. The band of pink, slick nylon that served as a border is all that remains of the covering. The rest has decomposed and vanished into the earth. But the bones are there. Splattered mud is stark against the white shape that lies almost fully intact like the skeletons you see hanging in a science classroom.

I blink. My backside hits the ground behind me as I stare at the bones.

Not an animal. Human bones. Bones that have been buried for a very long time.

Terror burns through my veins. I know these bones.

Noooo reverberates around me like the wind, buffeting my being. I jerk my head up to see where the soul shattering sound is coming from and it is only then that I realize the screams are coming from me. I scramble out of the pit, my head spinning.

The next thing I know I'm running…running toward the house. I rush inside, fly up the stairs, mud on my shoes causing me to slip. I scramble onward, toward my room. I need to be in my room—the one where I slept my whole life. The place where my history is documented from birth until just before my father died when he hung a photo of the two of us above the lamp on the bedside table.

I remember that day as clearly as if were yesterday.

What is happening to me?

I stare at the photo, our smiling faces. This is who I am. Whatever is wrong with me, isn't about that...can't be about my family. I close the door, sag against it to catch my breath. When my body stops trembling I look at the wooden doorframe to my left and the tick marks my parents posted there each time they measured my height from the time I was old enough to stand on my own. Happy laughter echoes in my head. My mother and I twirl-ing around the room.

This is *my* room...my space. My history. *My life.*

I go to the bookcase above the desk where I did homework as a kid. I grab a photo album and stare at the pictures of my parents and me. My muddy fin-gers flip through the pages. I stare at photo after photo. It's all there. All the memories in my head are right here on these pages.

The pain shears through my head and I stagger, close my eyes.

Not again.

The stabbing pain intensifies. I squeeze my eyes shut more tightly. Drop the photo album and stumble to my bed. I curl up on the soft, familiar comforter and pull a pillow over my head.

If I'm very, very still...keep my eyes closed tight... maybe it will pass.

THE CHILD

"There he is."

He was practically slobbering at the mouth like a wild dog as he watched the small boy. Skinny kid, maybe nine or ten years old. Mexican or something like that. He was kicking a ball down the sidewalk. No one else around. I figured he must be on his way home from a friend's. Most kids have friends.

But not me. I'm an *it*.

"What do you want him for?" I asked, an uncertainty growing inside me.

I couldn't keep the resentment out of my voice. I tried. I really did. It wasn't that I gave one shit about this bastard anymore, but I guess it was about survival. This boy—this new kid—was the person who would take my place.

The bastard behind the wheel no longer wanted me. I could tell. And I was glad, sort of. I had made up my mind that he would not hurt me again. I was leaving the first chance I got. But now he wanted someone new to rut. Someone to use to make himself feel good and powerful.

He wanted this boy. A boy, I knew, couldn't get pregnant. A boy wouldn't have the blood—the girl teaching me to read called it the rag. Having a boy would be a lot easier.

I shouldn't have cared.

But somehow I did.

"I want you to go talk to him."

I stared at him as if he had lost his mind. He'd made me play lookout plenty of times when he picked up kids, but not in a long time. Not since that one girl asked if I was his daughter. "Why do I have to talk to him?"

"Talk him into going into that house over there," he explained. "Tell him you dropped your cell phone and your arm is too fat to reach through the crack and get it. Tell him you'll pay him." He dug a five-dollar bill out of his pocket.

I stare at the money. "I can't do that."

He backhanded me, knocked me against the window. "Do it now before he's gone or I'll make you wish you had!"

My face stinging almost as much as my pride, I scrub away a telltale tear. "Whatever."

I got out of the car, closed my door quietly and then went around the bumper. Since the front door of the old house was standing open, getting in wouldn't be a problem. I hurry up the sidewalk until I'm even with the house, then I shout at the kid.

He stops, his red and blue ball held tightly in his hands. He stares at me, his face full of uncertainty.

"I don't mean to bother you." I smile real big as I hustle across the street toward him. "Can you help me a minute?"

The boy glances around as if looking for someone to ask if it's okay to talk to me.

"Don't be afraid. I just need someone with skinnier arms to help me get my cell phone." I point to the house. "I've been staying in there because I have no place else to go and my phone fell into a crack in the floor and my arm is too big to reach it. Can you get it for me?" I pull the money out of my pocket. "I'll pay you."

He glances at the five-dollar bill and then nods. "Okay."

It was so easy. The stupid kid did exactly what I told him except when we got in the house *he* was waiting. He pressed the cloth in his hand over the boy's mouth and the kid passed out. He told me to watch him while he got the car.

As I waited, I stared at the boy who looked even smaller lying on the floor. "Sorry," I muttered.

We took him to our place. He cried and cried and cried. I watched the way the man who had been my only family all this time touched this boy. I knew he wouldn't wait long to rut him. But he was holding off for some reason. Probably prolonging the foreplay or something. The girl who was teaching me to read said some guys liked that part better than the fucking—that's what she called the rutting.

Finally, when the boy just kept whining he got mad. He told me to watch him and that he'd be right back. I think he was going to get some liquor. I remembered he did that to me. Had me drink it so I wouldn't whine so much. He was probably going to do that to the boy.

I sat stone still on the tattered old chair and watched him huddled in the corner, his hands and feet bound, the gag in his mouth. I remembered being tied up just like that before he started putting me in the trunk and then the box. It wasn't this place. It was somewhere else. But he had done the same thing to me. Tonight, after he got enough liquor into the boy he would fuck him.

I would be forced to listen…to remember.

Then the boy would look at me with those big brown eyes and he would blame me because I was the one who trapped him.

No.

I was not going to be a prisoner any longer and I was not going to be the reason this boy lived the kind of life I had lived.

Hell no.

I was suddenly so angry and yet I was terrified. How would I do this? Thinking it was one thing, but where would I go? Could I really take care of myself?

I thought of my new friend and I realized I could haunt a street corner just like her. I could survive the same way she did.

I went over to the boy. He drew away as if he feared I would hurt him.

"I'm sorry I helped him catch you."

He sobbed, snot running down his skinny face.

"I'm going to help you but you have to promise me something first."

He stared into my eyes, the sobs fading to a hiccup.

"When he comes back I'm going to knock him out and then let you loose. You'll have to run for help. Tell the police what he did to you so they'll arrest him. But you can't tell them about me. Promise?"

His head bobbed up and down like one of those crazy street beggars on crack.

"Okay. But if you break that promise I will come back in the middle of the night and…"

He shook his head fast back and forth.

"We have a deal then. You just sit right there and be quiet. When he gets here you start your whining again. I'll be ready."

I didn't have much. Two pairs of jeans. The shoes I wore. A second pair of socks and panties and one other t-shirt. I packed all of it into a plastic bag from the supermarket. Then I remembered my teddy bear. It was the one thing I'd had for as long as I could remember, so I put it with the bag. I hid them behind the ragged couch.

In the kitchen there was no knife. He never left stuff like that lying around. But in the very back under the sink there was one of those big old forks—the kind people used for barbecuing. I guess the people who lived here before us had a grill. I took the big fork and tucked it between the cushion and the sofa arm and sat down to wait.

Half an hour passed with me and the kid just sitting there waiting for him to return. I was pretty sure the kid had shit himself since I smelled something bad. I couldn't risk helping him clean up because I needed to be in position for when the monster returned.

Finally, he unlocked the front door and came in, a paper sack in his arms. "Got you something, too," he announced, grinning at me. He pulled out a bottle of Coke and a bag of chips. "I thought you might want to go next door and watch TV."

We often heard the girl next door's television playing. He didn't know that I watched it sometimes when I went over there for my lessons.

"Okay," I said.

He put the bag down on the sofa next to me. "Me and the boy are going to bed now. He's tired." He slid the pint of liquor into his back pocket and turned toward the boy. "Smells like you need a bath."

I watched for a moment, the racket the kid was making growing as he sobbed louder and louder. The piece of shit bent to touch him and that's when I moved. My fingers curled around the handle of the big fork and I rammed it into him as hard as I could.

He screamed, jerked away from me.

The fork still grasped in both hands, I jumped back as he twisted around. His eyes were big and round and he was staring at me as if he intended to kill me.

He dove at me. I thrust the fork forward, ramming it into his gut this time. He just stood there staring at me. I pushed harder, driving the fork as deep as I could.

He crumpled to the floor but he started to rant at me. Screaming that he was going to kill me. I had to do something!

I grabbed the old ceramic lamp from the table. Jerked its cord free of the wall and crashed it as hard as I could over his head.

He collapsed onto his back and stopped moving...stopped making sounds.

My heart was in my throat. I crouched next to him and reached into his pocket in search of the knife he carried. I knew he had one. I had seen it before. I dug until I found it. My hands shaking, I ran to the boy and cut him loose. I pulled the balled up sock out of his mouth.

Before he could take off I grabbed him by the hand and pulled him toward the monster on the floor. His feet dragged and he cried as if he feared I was going to back out on our deal.

"Shut up," I snarled. I reached down and pulled the fork out of the bastard's gut. Blood dripped from its two points. He still didn't move. He might be dead.

I didn't care. I hoped he was.

"Take this," I ordered. The boy took hold of the bloody fork with both hands, the same way I had held it when I stabbed the bastard. "Go outside and start screaming. Throw this on the sidewalk so people see it and know something bad happened in here. Then run down the street screaming for help. Don't stop until someone calls the police. They have to call the police. Do you understand?"

He nodded frantically.

"If the police don't come he'll get away and find you again. You have to tell them what he did to you and that you stabbed him to get away. Understand?"

He nodded again, big tears rolling down his cheeks.

"You can't tell them about me, remember?"

Another bob of his head.

I got my bag and my teddy bear from behind the couch. "Go!"

I watched a moment as he ran out the door. He threw the big fork onto the sidewalk just like I told him and started to scream for help.

I dared to breathe, and then I turned to go.

Harsh fingers wrapped around my ankle.

My heart stuttered to a near stop. I fell face forward. My bag and teddy bear flew from my hands.

"You fucking bitch!"

I twisted around and kicked him in the face with my free foot. He howled and his fingers released me. I grabbed my shit and ran.

That was the last time I saw the monster that stole my life...until one week ago.

DETECTIVE WALTER DUNCAN

Mario Sanchez arrived home at eight this morning. He and his buddies drove through the night to be home in time to rest and prepare for a birthday party this afternoon. One of his pals is turning thirty.

Sanchez shows me to his private study. To be so young he's earned a surprising number of awards from the firm where he works. Other than the gram-toting beautician, all of Fanning's victims have done fairly well for themselves despite the horror of their childhoods. Even the beautician didn't do so badly. We all have bad habits. Mine is killing me. This very second the cancer is eating away at the tissue of my lungs. Every day less and less of that tissue works. One day they will stop working entirely and I will die.

Who am I to judge?

"So," Sanchez says once we are seated around his desk, "how can I help you with this investigation? I'm assuming since you're here that you haven't found Fanning."

I shake my head. "Not yet. You're the last of his victims we have to interview."

Sanchez nods. "I get the impression you believe someone on that list went after him, maybe harmed him in some way."

The guy would have to be a fool not to see that sticking out on a stem.

Rather than waiting for my answer, he goes on, "My mother told me how you questioned her about my whereabouts at the time of his disappearance. My wife said the same."

I shrug. "It's my job. Did you and your friends take him to Mexico and bury him?"

Sanchez laughs. "I can't say that I wouldn't have enjoyed doing just that, but no, we didn't. I haven't seen or heard from that bastard since the trial. If the world is lucky no one will ever hear from him again."

"Have you and any of the other victims ever gotten together and discussed Fanning?"

Sanchez shakes his head no. "I wanted to stay as clear of those memories as possible."

Sanchez's wife appears with two glasses of iced tea. Her rounded belly makes me think of Liv. I hope she can work things out for the best. Whatever that might be.

"I feel like there's something you want to ask me, Detective Duncan."

I smile. Perceptive guy. "You know, I read over your statements again this morning. The ones you made when you were ten years old and then your testimony at the trial. It was very practiced. You told your story carefully, ensuring all bases were covered, but it feels like you left something out."

His eyebrows rear up. "Really. My lawyer and the district attorney seemed to think my testimony was powerful. You know, unimpeachable."

"That's true. Maybe it's just me." I look him directly in the eyes. "I feel like there's something else you need to tell me." I shrug. "I don't know. Maybe it's the fact that you were a skinny ten-year-old. Little for your age. And you bested a forty-something-year-old-guy who was experienced in handling kids—each one of them larger than you. You not only bested him, you left him in bad shape. How did you manage to do that?"

He stares at me, unmoving. "You read the court transcripts. The statements I made to the police. You should know the answer."

"You had help, didn't you?" I'm on one hell of a fishing expedition and I'm just hoping he'll take the bait. My gut, every instinct I've got, tells me he had assistance escaping that bastard.

"Maybe I got lucky." He turns his hands up. "Maybe Fanning had a bad day. Who knows?"

"What was your relationship with Dr. Lewis Newhouse?"

His expression closes. "Detective, I think—"

"Whatever secret you're keeping, Mr. Sanchez," I cut him off, can't let him take that path, "you're not helping anyone. I need you to be straight with me. Lives depend on what happens next."

He smirks. "You mean Fanning's life?"

Anger flares. I let him see it. "Not just his. There are others who are hanging by their fingernails here. I need your help. Now. And you're wasting my time."

Silence swells between us for a moment. I see the change in his face when the tide of his emotions shifts in my direction.

"I've never told anyone this," he confesses. "She asked me not to tell and I didn't. I owed her my life and I wasn't about to let her down. Do you understand the position I was in as a child? She literally saved my life."

"Who?" My heart is racing. "I need a name."

He shakes his head. "I have no idea. I never knew her name. When Fanning took me, he didn't just take me to some parking lot or rundown building to rape me. He took me home. He was going to keep me. He said as much."

That part is news as well. "Go on."

"He already had another kid, a girl he'd been keeping. I don't know for how long. But she was older than me. I think maybe he was done with her and wanted someone younger. She must have sensed this and decided we both needed rescuing. She is the one who put him down so we could escape. She made me promise never to tell anyone about her. I think she was afraid the police would blame her for what he'd done."

Goddammit, I need more than that. "He never called her by name?"

Sanchez shook his head. "He called her *it*. She had this old ragged teddy bear." He shudders visibly.

"She was pale and her clothes were tattered and dirty. It was horrible. But she saved my life and I made a promise to keep her secret."

"I understand." I make a decision quickly. "You have my word that I will keep this between the two of us, but I need more information. If I have a sketch artist come—now—do you think you could describe her in detail?"

He smiles, his dark eyes bright with emotion. "I will never forget what she looked like. She was my superhero, always will be. You don't need to call anyone. I've drawn pictures of her my whole life."

Anticipation has me stretching over his desk as he digs through a drawer. He pulls out a sketchpad and flips it open to a page.

"This is the last one I did. I was thinking of her when Fanning was released last month."

I stare at the young girl's face. She looks vaguely familiar. I mentally run down the list of Fanning's victims. She doesn't look like any of them. "Can I keep this for a while?"

He nods. "If it will help, yes."

I meet his gaze and consider for a long moment if I really want to know the answer to my next question. "This is important. I need a straight answer. How did you know Dr. Newhouse?"

He lets out a long, low breath. "Just before the trial he talked to me after school one day. I thought he was just another of the doctors the police insisted I see, but he said no. He came to speak to me about something different." Sanchez stares at his hands for a moment. "He told me if I stuck with my story and never told anyone about the girl that he would pay for me to go to college anywhere I wanted to go." He laughs. "I thought he was bullshitting me, but he wasn't. Even before I graduated high school he had already made all the financial arrangements. Even sent a letter of recommendation for me. He did exactly what he said he'd do. The funny thing is, he didn't have to. I would never have told anyone about her anyway. I made a promise and I intended to keep it."

The realization hits me then, shakes me to the very core of my being. I draw in a hard breath. Swallow back the denial burgeoning in my throat. "Did Newhouse mention why he wanted to protect this girl? Was she a patient of his?"

Sanchez shakes his head. "I have no idea. Looking back, I guess that's the only reasonable explanation. I learned later that Newhouse was a major donor to a number of organizations that help children who are victims of abuse. I guess maybe it was personal somehow for him."

"You never heard from him again?" My pulse is tripping. I can't find my footing with the theory swelling in my brain.

Sanchez looks away for a moment before he answers. "I hadn't heard from him in all those years until he contacted me back in January. He said we needed to talk about a couple of things. First, he warned me that Fanning's release date was coming up and that I should beware. Dr. Newhouse feared the bastard would try to seek revenge. But I figured Fanning was just a sad old man incapable of hurting anyone anymore. Just in case, I had a new security system installed at my house and sent my wife to her mother's in Memphis while I was gone to Mexico."

Whatever else Fanning said to Newhouse, this confirms the doc had reason to suspect the bastard might reach out to some of his victims. "What was the other thing he wanted to talk to you about?"

His gaze searched mine for a long moment. "He wanted to make sure our deal remained in effect. He said he'd heard I was having a kid. He set up a college fund for my unborn child." New tears bloom in his eyes. "I know Dr. Newhouse is dead but I feel like I am betraying him now. He was good to me. I kept my promise to him until this moment. Do you see why we can never tell anyone?"

I nod. "I think I do." I push my weary body from the chair. "I'll get this back to you, Mr. Sanchez."

I say goodbye to his wife and walk out of the house. All that he told me—the face he has drawn—whirl in my head. As I reach my Tahoe my cell vibrates against my side. I climb behind the wheel as I answer it. I hope it's Liv and that she had a better night last night. I called her before I came to meet with Sanchez but her cell went straight to voicemail. I need to see her. To talk to her…this idea expanding in my mind can't be right.

Can't be. Can't be.

"Hey, Detective, it's Reynolds."

It might be Sunday but cops don't have the luxury of being off duty just because it's the Lord's Sabbath.

"Hey, Reynolds. You get that other report?"

I start the engine but don't move. We've been waiting on the DNA results on the second blood type found in Fanning's duplex. I'm assuming that's why Reynolds has called. I'm praying it will take this damn theory nagging at me in a whole different direction.

I need it to go a different way.

"Sure did and you are not going to believe what the lab report says. I'm thinking they got this one mixed up with that case a couple years back when all those cops got injured by that strung-out perp. You might not remember but we had to separate out all the blood types, perform DNA tests, it was a real mess."

My heart sinks.

"Anyway," Reynolds goes on, "I'm standing here staring at the lab report on that second blood type from your crime scene and I'm certain this can't be right. There has to be a mix-up. Some kind of wacky mistake."

But I know it's not a mistake.

DETECTIVE OLIVIA NEWHOUSE

I woke in my childhood room. The pain was gone but so was a part of me that I fear I will never get back.

I crawled from the bed, across the plush carpet and picked up the photo album. There, on every page, are my memories. Each memory of my life burned into my brain came from these photos... from the stories my parents told me.

But none of it ever happened...to *me*.

A halting breath shudders through my chest as I lay the album aside, get to my feet and do next what I know I must.

I walk out of the house and keep going until I stand before the barn that once housed beautiful horses. Dr. Lewis Newhouse told me about all the graceful creatures that once grazed in the pastures surrounding his home. His wife, Corrine, was an internationally famous equestrian in American dressage. Once upon a time her trophies lined the walls of their home. But it was their child, their beautiful, sweet daughter, they hoped to groom for Olympic competition.

I draw in a heavy breath. There once was a child named Olivia Newhouse. Her parents protected her so carefully from the ugliness of the world that her prestigious and lettered father experienced in his work every day. She had private tutors, never once attended school outside her home. Everywhere Olivia went her mother or a cautiously chosen and carefully vetted Nanny was sure to go. And still Olivia, at the tender young age of eleven, encountered her first taste of drugs. For the next two years she sneaked behind her loving parents' backs and found a way to fulfill this new need that throbbed relentlessly inside her.

But then her parents discovered her dark secret and the real trouble began. Olivia was under house arrest, not allowed to see or to communicate with anyone. One night she decided she no longer wanted to live that way so Olivia swallowed a whole bottle of her mother's secret stash of sleeping pills.

When she was found, unresponsive and barely breathing, she was rushed to the hospital. But the damage was done. Olivia's heart continued to beat with assistance but her brain was already dead. In time, Dr. and Mrs. Newhouse took their beloved brain dead child home and made her as comfortable as possible. No matter that a machine was required to keep her breathing and that Dr. Newhouse was well versed in the science of what had occurred, they hoped and prayed that the specialists were wrong and that one day she would open her beautiful blue eyes and come back to them.

But she never did.

Each day for two long years Corrine drew more deeply into herself. The beautiful horses were neglected and eventually sold. Dr. Newhouse gave up his practice. They sat in the quiet house day in and day out, listening to the wheeze of the machine keeping their daughter alive and waiting for a miracle that was not going to come.

Dr. Newhouse decided he had to do something or he would lose his precious Corrine as well. He thought of all the young girls who lived on the streets of the city. The ones whose parents had forsaken them...the ones whom society had let down. He began searching the streets until he found exactly the girl he was looking for. A girl with the blond hair and blue eyes of his precious Olivia. A girl the right height who could, with the proper grooming and education, become his sweet Olivia and fulfill the life she had been destined to live. But this child had been damaged by another man—a monster—and it took time for Dr. Newhouse to convince her to trust him. Finally, she did. She climbed into his car and allowed him to take her to the farm he had told her all about...to the woman waiting to be her new mother.

That was the day I, the Child who once belonged to a monster, became Olivia Newhouse.

My new father took the *it* Joseph Fanning had created and polished her into the perfect daughter. I stare toward the woods and the grave I opened last night. The real Olivia Newhouse was buried there once the machine keeping her body alive was turned off. My new father waited until my transition was complete, then he told me that it was time for the child in the bed to have peace. I remember thinking she was like Sleeping Beauty except no prince was coming to wake her. Her brain was dead and no force on this earth could bring her back.

But she could be replaced.

By then I hardly remembered my former life. During those long months of grooming and educating, I didn't understand that I was being reprogrammed. Though my father meant well and certainly saved me from a life on the streets and perhaps a horrible death, what he did was ultimately brainwashing. Using hypnosis and other techniques, he slowly replaced my bad memories with good ones—with Olivia's memories. I can tell you everything about her and her parents...about this place and the lives they lived here. The vacations they took... *everything.*

But I do not know my real name. I don't remember my biological parents.

Until one month ago the name Joseph Fanning meant nothing to me. I saw his face on the news during his highly publicized release from prison, but the name and image of the man barely registered in my brain. My new father did a very good job of scrubbing him from my memory.

I now know that one week ago my subconscious started trying to recreate those awful memories in an effort to prompt me to protect myself. I had no idea I was being watched by pure evil. But my most basic instincts recognized that danger hovered close by. Fanning was watching me. I saw him more than once, but he had disguised himself and the recognition didn't click. The human mind is a very complex thing. It hides the details that one cannot bear to face. Denial is one of the strongest human emotions that exist. I saw what I wanted to see and ignored all the rest.

But those deeply entrenched survival instincts from my early childhood combined with the enhanced protective hormones of pregnancy ultimately proved stronger than my denial. They kicked in and the child I once was emerged. All those times in the past week that I crashed into the blackness of an intense migraine, went utterly unconscious into what felt like a black hole, the child I used to be resurfaced...did what had to be done. Even in my dreams, sometimes the memories seeped through. But each time I awoke, the carefully programmed adult me took over and denial did the rest.

Then, a few days ago during the aura—those awful minutes before a debilitating migraine kicks in—the memories came crashing back in spurts of ugly images and awful words and this time some of them lingered. The denial was fighting a losing battle. This very minute, more are filtering through the carefully constructed membrane of protection the only real father I have ever known helped to put in place in my damaged mind. I assume these memories are of actual events but I can't be certain. So much is still unclear.

I don't remember my name but I am the child Joseph Fanning raped and abused for eight long years. I am the *it* whose universe was filled only by him and what he wanted. Of this much I am certain.

I open the barn door and step inside. Even after all these years it still smells of hay and horses. My heart quickens. I've had flashes of memories about him being chained and, after discovering the bones I dug up, more snippets of memory seeped into my head. Images of me torturing him. I shudder.

I find the switch for the lights, flip it and then move deeper into the enormous structure. The tack room is on the right. My mother's trophies and ribbons as well as those of the child who's buried in the woods are neck deep in that room. All the horse gear was sold along with the horses.

At the end of the row, in the very last stall, I find him. He is chained to the far wall, to the ring meant for a horse's reins. The smell of feces and urine and death fill my lungs. My first impulse is to go to him and see if he's still alive, but I resist. I will not go near him. I hope he's dead.

Whispers of words, flickers of images sift through my mind. Finding the note he left on the windshield of my car while I was in the house going through my father's papers. *I'm waiting in the barn.* Me walking toward the barn, agony spearing through my brain with every step I made. Bringing water to him and even food on one occasion. I haven't tended

233

his wound, that's obvious, but I haven't killed him either. Perhaps my dedication to the oath I took prevented me from crossing that line.

The calmness I feel surprises me. I'm not sure what I should be feeling but I'm certain this is not it. As an officer of the law it's my duty to serve and protect, yet I cannot bring myself to do either for him.

His eyes open and the corners of his split lips lift upward. "I didn't think you were coming back this time."

"How did you get here?" I steel my spine and force my brain to shift into cop mode. I might not know the name I was given at birth but I am still a cop. On the floor between us is the balled up piece of paper—his note. I should pick it up; it's evidence. But that would mean moving closer to him. I can't be certain of his restraint.

He laughs, the sound dry and rotten as if his throat is ripping apart. "Why you brought me here at gunpoint, don't you remember?"

My head moves from side to side. "No. You brought yourself here." I'm hoping like hell I can trick him into telling me what actually happened. I have no idea beyond the vague memory of finding that note, but every instinct I possess screams in denial of what he suggests.

Yet, I know denial all too well.

Perhaps *I* have become the monster. Perhaps there wasn't a note. I glance at the wadded up paper again. But there it is.

"Well maybe you did and maybe you didn't," he says on a wheeze, drawing my attention back to him, "but what do you think your friends in the police department are going to think? You wouldn't be the first cop to crack, particularly under the circumstances. If you tell them the sad, sad story of your life, maybe they'll feel sorry for you and send you to one of those cushy mental hospitals instead of to prison. Either way, you're going down, girl."

I refuse to fear him or anything he can do to me. The image of a baby being taken from me arrows into my head, rips through my heart. I flinch. I push that memory away and consider that his words suggest that *he* wants the police to think I'm responsible for all this. More evidence that he is behind the whole set up.

He laughs again. "Newhouse took you and turned you into something you could never really be. I told him that deep down you were still mine. I branded you at seven years old. He couldn't wash that away."

I can imagine how the man who raised me—the only father who ever really loved me—felt at hearing those foul words. "You were wrong."

"If you're so changed, what am I doing here dying like this?"

"You don't sound as if you're dying."

"Oh I'm dying all right. But I'm taking you to hell with me."

"Obviously you aren't clever enough to make that happen." The longer we talk, the more convinced I become of one thing: I know this piece of shit. If I goad him hard enough, he will spill his guts. "You never were very bright."

"It was so easy." He grins at me like the devil he is. "I saw you and that cowboy partner of yours on the news. I recognized you instantly, and I knew despite all the polish and highfalutin education that deep down you're still my little girl. My heart pounded so hard I lost my breath, got hard just thinking about you. Right then and there, I called my attorney. Made sense he wouldn't want nothing to do with me unless there was something in it for him so I told him my plan. Let's just say he was intrigued. All he had to do was dig up everything he could find on Lewis and Corrine Newhouse and their lovely daughter, *Olivia.*"

I want to vomit. To scream. But I need him to keep talking, to explain what the hell he means. I have to know what happened during all those blackouts I experienced this week. "You see," I taunt, "I knew you weren't smart enough to plot all this on your own."

He attempted to laugh but coughed instead. "Oh, but after he gave me the lowdown, I figured out all the rest from there. Planned every last detail, and I knew that once we spent some time together you would want to hurt me. All I had to do was set things in motion."

I lift my chin and stare directly into his beady eyes. "I guess you weren't expecting that I'd forgotten all about you and the life we shared. Until just now, I didn't even know you were here."

Another of those dry laughs ripped from his throat. "Yeah, right. You're lying just like he did. Newhouse told me you weren't that child anymore, that you didn't remember anything from the past. He begged me to let you go. He was so sincere, so worried that I would hurt you again that he just kept upping the ante. So I took the money he offered for my silence. He turned it over to my attorney and I put him right to work on part two of my plan. By the time Dr. Newhouse came back to the prison for a final meeting I knew all his secrets. I knew his wife was dead and that you weren't this Olivia you were strutting around claiming to be. I guess that chat kind of tore him up 'cause he dropped dead of that heart attack a few days later."

I roar with outrage, rush toward him determined to finish off what is left of his pathetic, shitty life.

He just laughs and laughs until he can't breathe and then he coughs and coughs. "The minute I got out," he clears his throat, "I started watching you. Went through your trash. That's how I got your blood. That night you cut yourself—you really should close the blinds in that swanky house—I watched you take the mess out to the trash. I took it, not sure exactly what I'd do with it, but a plan was coming together."

I think of the second blood type found at the scene. "You planted my DNA in that shithole you call home."

"Pretty fucking brilliant for a not so bright nothing like me."

"Too bad you just confessed to a police detective."

"They'll never believe you. Not after all the bizarre shit you've done this week. I'm sure your hot-shot fiancé thinks you're crazy as hell already. You told me that yourself. I don't think you meant to. You came in here muttering and talking to yourself. I swear, you even had me convinced you'd lost it. Between me and Newhouse, we done mind fucked you up good, girl."

I ignore his crude words. What he thinks is irrelevant to me. "I know what you did, Fanning. You set this whole thing up. You want me to take the fall for your murder. That's your way of getting revenge, isn't it?"

"Now you're getting the picture." He smirks.

I want to beat that smirk off his twisted face.

"I had a different plan at first, you wouldn't have liked it any better, trust me. But you see, right after I was released from prison I found out I have AIDS. Full blown. Hell, that damn prison hospital probably knew it but didn't tell me just to keep from having to take care of me. I was so close to my release date, they just kept that little secret to themselves and let me find out all on my own. The clinic says I can't take the medicine I need because of all the other shit that's wrong with me. So, you see, I'm a dead man anyway. Even if this," he tugs at his restraints, "is cutting my time a little short, it's worth it to have sweet revenge before I go."

Now I understand what my father was doing looking up information on the victims and visiting him in prison. Fury twists inside me. My fists clench with the need to tear his head off.

"Making you angry, am I? Too bad. You're the reason I went to prison. If I hadn't gone, I wouldn't have contracted this shit. All these years you've had it made. Been treated like a princess. Now, you're going to pay for what you did to me."

"Well." I nod, my brain too weary to process reasonable thoughts anymore. "I guess there's only one thing left I can do."

He grins up at me as if he can't wait for me to come at him. The bastard wants to die. Wants me to pay the price for killing him.

I laugh. Not today. "Goodbye, you piece of shit."

DETECTIVE WALTER DUNCAN

The tires squeal as I slam to a stop in front of Preston's house. I jump out of my Tahoe and rush to the front door and start pounding. I need to find Liv. She isn't answering her cell. I'm worried. Worried sick.

This whole idea is wrong. Not possible. And yet I know there is no other reasonable explanation.

The rattle of the lock and the swing of the door opening sends renewed tension through my muscles. Preston stares at me. "If you're looking for Liv, she's not here."

"Do you know where she is?"

"I have no fucking clue." He walks away, leaving the door open.

It's not until then that I notice the box cutter in his hand. A frown nags at my brow. The stack of boxes I helped Liv move from her place still stands to one side in the entry hall. Preston zips the box cutter along the taped edges of the box closest to him.

Since he left the door open, I take it as an invitation. "Are you saying you haven't seen her today?"

"Oh yeah, I saw her." He puts the potential weapon aside and reaches for the flaps of the box. "I woke up in bed with a woman covered in mud from the waist down. She's fucking lost it." He shakes his head, laughs the sound of defeat. "I have no idea what's happening."

I wonder if he knows she's carrying his child. The urge to beat the shit out of him is nearly overpowering. Instead, I take a breath and follow my cop instincts. "Where did the mud come from?"

"You tell me." The words are high pitched, oozing with frustration. "She first said it was from a crime scene." He stares at me as if he believes I already know all this. "Then she said that was a lie so I have no idea."

I take another breath, again resist the urge to pound his high and mighty ass. "How long ago did she leave?"

"Maybe two, two and a half hours ago." He pauses and looks at the grandfather clock in the corner. "It's eleven now. I got up at seven-thirty. Saw the mud and freaked out. She showered and left. I'm pretty sure she was out of here by eight-thirty, maybe quarter of nine." He shakes his head again. "I don't know. She's gone over some edge or something."

The claws of worry dig deeper. "You have no idea where she went?"

"I figured she went to you." He turns to face me. "She seems to care more about your feelings than mine."

I got no time to deal with his ridiculous suspicions. "Clearly, she isn't with me. You think she went to the farm?"

He shrugs. "Probably. She apparently doesn't want to be here." He reaches into the box and pulls out an object. "What the hell is this?"

The ragged old teddy bear confirms what I can no longer deny.

I'm on my way out the door as I shout back to him, "I'll let you know when I find her."

Driving like a crazy man, it takes the longest twenty-five minutes of my life to reach the farm. Liv's car is there. The tight band around my chest loosens a fraction. I check her car. Her wallet and cell phone are on the console. I frown at the mud. The fiancé was right. Mud on the floorboard and some in the driver's seat.

I rush to the house, pound on the door and it flies inward. My heart drops. I reach for my weapon and enter the house slowly.

Scanning the great room, I move to the right, check the library and workout room, then head for the hall beyond the kitchen. Laundry room, her father's office and downstairs bedroom are clear. En suite bath is clear. Closets are clear.

I rush up the stairs. Spot mud on the carpet. Damn. But no Liv. Her bed looks as if she slept in it. Photo albums are scattered on the floor. There's mud on the rug, on some of the pages in the photo album. "Where the hell are you, Liv?"

Back outside, I scan the yard. I check the garage and the garden shed which are the only outbuildings near the house. No Liv.

My gaze shifts to the barn.

That's when I start running, my weapon palmed.

I reach the barn, my chest wheezing, pain radiating through me like an electrical current. Inside, the overhead lights are on. Florescent fixtures suspended below the hayloft, showering the stalls with light. I check the tack room, nothing but piles of trophies. I remember that Liv and her mother were big into horse shows.

That denial I've been hanging onto hardens into a bitter ball in my gut.

One by one I check the stalls. The smell of human feces sifts into the lingering scent of hay and earth as I near the rear of the barn. My heart rate climbs as I grow closer and closer to the final stall. The gate is already open. I line up with the open space and stare at the naked man chained to the back wall.

His head droops forward. A gaping pus filled gash stretches down the upper part of his right arm. Bruises are stark against his gray skin. I move closer. See the shallow rise and fall of his chest. He's alive.

I crouch down and take a look at his face. Definitely Fanning. His lids flutter open. He's in bad shape.

His cracked lips spread into a smile. "I got her."

Son of a bitch.

To avoid finishing him off, I push to my feet and turn away. The logical part of me wants to reach for my cell and call it in but I can't do that. Not until I know what the hell is going on here…

Not until I know the truth.

I'm all the way outside in the sun before I realize I've been holding my breath. The air pours into my aching lungs as I walk back toward the house. I see Liv sitting on the front porch steps. My heart twists with an agony that far exceeds the pain in my failing lungs. As I reach her I notice the shovel propped against the porch next to her. Her shoes are muddy as hell, as are her jeans. I want to grab her and hug her, to promise her everything will be all right, but first I have to know the whole story.

I have to find a way to protect her.

I muster up a calm face and sit down beside her. "I was looking for you."

"I was in the woods. There was something I needed to do."

She stares at her open palms and I flinch at the bloody blisters there. The thousand knots already in my gut twist a little tighter.

"That's where the bones Fanning was muttering about are buried. I had to make sure her remains were covered. To protect them until…" She meets my gaze then. "Until she can be moved to the cemetery where her parents are buried."

Liv falls silent then, her attention shifting out to the barn.

"So," every ounce of strength I possess is required to keep my voice calm and steady, "you want to talk about it?"

She exhales a big breath. "I don't even know where to begin." She looks at me again, her blue eyes full of uncertainty. "You should arrest me now, Walt. And call a bus for that piece of shit out in the barn, assuming he isn't dead yet."

"He's still breathing." I reach for my phone. "I'll call EMS and have an ambulance dispatched and then you tell me the parts I need to know starting with how Fanning got in your barn."

I have a feeling that part is going to make all the difference in how this ends.

FRIDAY, MAY 25

DETECTIVE OLIVIA NEWHOUSE

"Detective Newhouse, the internal affairs investigation has confirmed that the deceased, Joseph Fanning, did indeed set out to frame you for his own murder. An unexpected and surprising new way, in my opinion, to commit suicide by cop. Based on the testimony of Fanning's attorney, Alexander Cagle, and that of your partner, Walter Duncan, the Internal Affairs investigation found no evidence of criminal behavior on your part. However, the matter of unprofessional behavior remains in question. Taking into consideration the conclusions in your psychiatric evaluation it is clear you were not aware of your interactions with Joseph Fanning after he imprisoned himself on your property; and, therefore, not criminally liable for those actions. However, that conclusion calls to question your mental fitness."

I wait for Lieutenant Weatherford to continue. This is a special hearing—not the usual review board or meeting with superiors—because this is an unusual situation. All involved, from the DA to

Internal Affairs and to my captain, have struggled with how to proceed. The past nineteen days have been the longest of my life.

"The review committee has weighed these conclusions as well as all the supporting documentation of this horror story that was your life, Detective Newhouse. We are prepared to proceed with a final determination on those findings; however, you have requested an opportunity to make an additional statement. Do you still feel so inclined, Detective?"

"I do, sir."

Weatherford nods. "Very well, please proceed."

I take a breath and begin. "My name is Olivia Newhouse. I am a detective with the Metro Nashville Police Department. Though Olivia Newhouse is my legal name, I am not Olivia Newhouse. Olivia Newhouse died at home when she was fifteen years old after being in a coma for two years.

"I have no idea what my real name is or who my parents were. The complete details of how I came to be Olivia Newhouse are in my statements which you have already reviewed." I brace to say the rest. What I am about to impart are the hardest words I have ever had to say aloud. "Though the Newhouses loved me—I'm certain of that—and they gave me a wonderful life, I realize now that I have actually been a prisoner twice in my life. First, to the monster who took a seven-year-old child and raped and abused her, and then to the parents of a dead girl who only wanted their daughter back. In both instances I was remade into what others wanted me to be. I can't be certain of the long-term ramifications to my mental stability. It was hardly more than three weeks ago that the buried memories began to resurface in the form of debilitating migraines."

The lieutenant raises a hand to stop me for a moment. "The psychiatrist who conducted your evaluation feels strongly that you are not mentally fit for field duty. He suggests an extended leave with continued counseling and eventually an administrative assignment. Have you had an opportunity to digest and come to terms with that evaluation?"

"Yes, sir. He's right." I pause for a moment, get right with the rest of what I need to say. "I wouldn't want to be my partner in the field. Though I feel fine and I've had no more migraines or blackouts, I no longer trust myself to be the backup a partner deserves in the field."

"Are you willing to accept an administrative assignment once the other conditions specified are met, Detective Newhouse?"

"Sir, with all due respect, it is my wish to resign and to step away from police work in any capacity for now."

A weight lifts from my shoulders as I say the words. Under the table, my hands press gently against my abdomen. I have other things that need my attention. There's the baby and I need to be there for Walt for whatever time he has left. And there's David.

I've thought long and hard about the future and decided that the greatest thing I can do for the memory of the man and woman who gave me their love and their security is to donate the farm to an organization that will turn it into a safe haven for abused children. The money the Newhouses left me will fund the transformation of the house as well as the operation for years to come. No matter that what they did was wrong, divisive even, their intent and the relationship that developed between us as the years passed was loving and generous.

I owe them my respect and my love.

After a final statement from the lieutenant, the hearing adjourns and hands are shaken. My captain holds onto my hand for an extra beat and tells me I will be missed. I thank him and he wishes me the best of luck.

I walk through the doors into the corridor where David and Walt are waiting for me.

David smiles and hugs me. "You okay?"

I inhale the scent of him, so very grateful that I didn't ruin our relationship with my secrets. My therapist has helped me to see that David's attempts to stop our relationship from falling apart triggered the child I once was to fight against the perceived domination. We have a long way to go to get where we need to be but this baby will need both of us.

I draw back from his hug and nod. "I am now."

"Good." David steps aside so Walt can give me a hug next.

"You did the right thing, kid." He glances at David. "We all did."

The three of us walk out together. Walt officially retired on Monday. For some time to come I'll be focused on the therapy I need and with taking care of Walt. David understands this and I genuinely appreciate his support. Later, he and I will revisit the possibility of marriage. Whatever else happens, we've agreed to raise this child together.

In addition to all the psychiatric testing I've endured the past two and a half weeks, I've had all the other necessary tests, including for HIV since I was in close contact with Fanning. So far so good, but that test will be repeated in two months and then again two months after that just to be sure.

But, I am moving forward. This is just the beginning of my new life.

The life I've led until now belonged to someone else. In truth, I suppose you could say I've died twice and been resurrected. This time *this* life will be mine. My goal is to figure out the motherhood thing so I can be the best mother possible for my child. I don't really know how normal people take care of normal children. I've never really been normal, certainly none of the people involved with the first three decades of my life could be labeled as normal.

I want this child to have a real *normal*...whatever that is.

I have no desire to find out who my biological parents were. They're dead. There's no point going back there. But the child, the baby boy, taken from me when I was fourteen is another story. I wanted to find him and I did. Actually, Fanning did. When my father gave the bastard's attorney all that money, one of the things that Fanning asked him to do was to locate the boy. Fanning intended to use him to hurt me. But his plan backfired. My son is a happy and healthy fifteen-year-old who lives in Brentwood. I met with his parents and explained everything. They are wonderful people, he is happy and I will not spoil that.

Maybe one day he'll want to know about me, but until then I want him to live his life without the shadow of my painful past.

In fact, that's exactly what I intend to do: move on without looking back.

There once was a child, frightened and alone, but that child grew up—I look from David to Walt—and I am definitely not alone.

CPSIA information can be obtained
at www.ICGtesting.com
Printed in the USA
LVOW10s2028180518
577692LV00002B/382/P